THE PATH IS THE WAY

Mohit Badoni

Become
Shakespeare
.com

This edition is published by BecomeShakespeare.com in 2015 in India, Sri Lanka, USA and UK

First published in 2015 by

BecomeShakespeare.com
Wordit Content Design & Editing Services Pvt Ltd
Quest Offices, C38/39,
Parinee Crescenzo Building, G Block,
Bandra Kurla Complex, Bandra East,
Mumbai 400 051, India
T: +91 8080226699

Cover Designer: Swastika Bist
Concept: Swati Joshi
Cover Picture Courtesy: Jayant Karna

ISBN 978-93-83952-42-7

For Gaurvi and Raghavi, good luck pigeons.

Part One

It is a slow sultry evening and the sun is touching the horizon. The game begins – the game of hide-and-seek, all my cousins and friends ready for action as soon as I start the count. Gudiya, Charu, Richu, Ami, Pooja, all hiding in the massive litchi and mango orchard.

'One, two, three…fifty…hundred. I'm ready.'

'He is coming.' The voices are dim, far away from some corner of the orchard. I know the orchard and their hiding places very well, but today I am unable to get there. The place seems unknown and I am searching every corner – behind the massive trees, up in the branches, between the rocks, but they are not there. I can hear them laugh but I can't find them. I start to panic. It is getting dark and the stories about evil spirits and the witch that live in that orchard are lingering on my mind.

'Come out, everyone! Gudiya, Charu, come out!' My heart is beating fast; I can hear the thumping of my heart. I want to shout and cry out loud; I am afraid of the dark – as always.

'Why don't you come out? I lose! You win! But please, come out!' I scream.

'Please come out, it's dark! I'm scared!' I can still hear them laugh and then there was a violent thud. It sounded like someone was banging a door with closed fists.

Knock…knock…knock!
'Ram-Ram, Saab, good evening, sir.'
Knock…knock…knock!
'Ram-Ram, Saab.'

The violent knock on my door woke me from my nightmare.

Someone was knocking my door, furiously and impatiently. I reached for my dressing-gown and opened the door, still half asleep. My buddy, rifleman Liccha Ram was at the door. Manzoor, one of the Special Operation Group (SOG) agents was there to meet me.

I quickly changed into my combat uniform and instructed my buddy to inform the senior JCO (Junior Commissioned Officer) *Subedar* Devi Singh Rathore and get the *ghataks* (commando team) ready. I knew Manzoor had credible inputs about Uzefa alias Abu Ali, code sign 77. He was hiding in Noor Mahi's house. I checked my watch, it displayed half-past midnight. The game of hide-and-seek which was haunting me, was about to begin.

The plan was quickly chalked out and the *ghataks* briefed about the location and sequence of action once we get there. Our first priority would be to cordon off the house before first light. I informed my Commanding Officer and asked for additional troops to establish the outer cordon. I knew this was my best chance to get Abu Ali alias Uzefa code sign 77, a self-styled district commander of the Pir Panjal Division, a well-known terrorist outfit.

We moved in the hours of darkness and by 04:00hrs, the target house was cordoned. By 05:00hrs, outer cordons were laid by the neighboring company. We waited for the first light to commence the search operation. I silently prayed to *Maa Durga*, Goddess of Strength to help me.

Ya Devi Sarva-bhuteshu,
Shakti-rupenu-sansthitaa,

Mohit Badoni

Namastasyae, Namastasyae, Namastasyae,
Namaho-namaha.

"O Mother, who is present everywhere,
who is the embodiment of Power and Energy,
I bow to you, I bow to you, I bow to you."

The morning had set in with a dim, faded light, which brightened as the clouds scattered. I could see a woman, probably thirty-years-old, but her stance resembling a woman approaching sixty. She came out of the solitary door with a steel bucket. The bucket had a prominent dent in the center and the shine of metal had faded after constant use. She was heading towards the nearby stream, possibly to fetch water for her household chores. Witnessing her house cordoned by soldiers, she got startled. The soldier covering the main entrance signaled her to keep quiet by putting an index finger on his lips. In a flash, she ran inside; she knew trouble was at her doorstep.

Precisely after two minutes, an old, battered man came out to confirm what he must have been told by his daughter-in-law. I waved my hand at him.

'*Janab,* Mister Noor Mahi, please come here.' He looked at me with grim eyes and then reluctantly, with trembling feet, he started moving towards me.

'*Janab,* we need to search your house. I would request you to please assist us in the search. Please tell all your family members to come out.'

'Yes, sir.' While he spoke in a faint, dead voice, he was shivering from head to toe, and droplets of sweat were visible on his forehead despite the cold morning. Slowly, he went inside, and we waited. But even after half an hour, no one came out. Manzoor's information was now authenticated beyond doubt.

I had been operating in this area and was well-versed with their traits. I knew soft words would not work, so I called the village headman and threatened that I want the house vacated in five minutes or else I would blow up the house and later they may complain to every human rights agency under the sun. Frantic announcements were made by the village headman and finally, Noor Mahi came out with his daughter-in-law and two children – a girl aged five and a boy aged seven.

I requested the village headman to take the woman and the children to a safe place and instructed my JCO to take a few men along with Noor Mahi and get the house searched thoroughly. After one hour, the JCO came out.

'*Saab*, no one is inside the house.' I wondered how that was possible. Was there some tunnel inside? I looked at Manzoor, his eyes telling me our prey was indeed inside. I decided to take a look myself. I strapped on my bulletproof jacket tight and moved inside with the search party.

I searched every inch of the house: cupboards, the cowshed, the kitchen, everywhere, but there were no telltale signs. Where the hell he could vanish? Frustrated, I gave up. Probably, his early warning elements must have given him a warning and he would have escaped before the cordon was laid. I started to move towards the door but as I was about to move out I saw a big trunk. I couldn't look away. There was something wrong, something unusual and my sixth sense was telling me to look at it carefully. Although my mind assured me that everything was okay, I had goosebumps. My body could sense the prevalent danger, particularly from the steel trunk three feet high and around four feet wide. There were clothes and quilts that seemed to be removed from the trunk and scattered around its base. The question that struck my mind was why did Noor Mahi leave the clothes on the floor when he could have placed them on the bed right next to it?

'Get that trunk removed!' I ordered.

'There is nothing inside the trunk, see it's empty.' There was fear in Noor Mahi's eyes, his voice was trembling.

'Take it out!' I shouted.

Two soldiers started to drag the trunk outside. Before I could have realized that there was something beneath the trunk, the *rut-a-tut* of an AK burst startled me. I knew two or three bullets had hit me in the stomach. I thanked my stars that the bulletproof jacket was on me. However, the kinetic energy of the bullets was transferred in my belly and it felt as if a stone had struck me there. I fell flat on my back.

Someone jumped out of the hidden trench beneath the trunk and ran outside. I could see him clearly: he was barefoot, holding an AK56 – foldable butt, barrel a little short. Then, the violent burst of a Light Machine Gun (LMG) was heard. I knew we'd got him, the door was covered by *Havildar* (Sergeant) Dharampal and he never misses.

I got up slowly, my stomach still hurting with a burning sensation. I placed my hand on it and tried to rub the location, when I realized something was wrong. I looked at my hand – it was crimson with gore. I had been hit; a bullet had pierced through the side of my bulletproof jacket. The bullet had possibly ricocheted off the wall and had entered through the side of my waist.

'Call the ambulance! *Saab* has been hit!' my buddy shouted. I sat on the floor, keeping my weapon to a side and resting my back against the wall. Slowly, I removed the bulletproof jacket and looked at my wound; I was bleeding profusely. The mere realisation that I had been hit was making me weak. Soon, a couple of soldiers rushed in with a stretcher, while my buddy tied a bandage on my wound. I carefully laid myself on the stretcher and closed my eyes. They carried me; I heard the ambulance door open.

I opened my eyes; the doctor's nametag was the most prominent thing visible to me. 'Shahid Hussain', his name in yellow letters on the nametag. He was talking to his nursing assistant.

'His blood pressure is going down, I think the bullet has perforated the liver, or probably a part of the lungs.'

I know it will be difficult; it was two hours to the base hospital.

'Doc, am I going to die?' I asked.

'Don't worry, just keep speaking to me', he said, piercing a long needle in my arm.

'Doc, can you save me?'

'I don't know, but if you go off to sleep, you will surely die. Just keep yourself awake. Keep talking to me. Talk about any damn thing.'

'Doc, is it worth it?'

'It is always better to live and do something for your country.'

'Then save me, doc.'

'If you want to live, keep yourself awake. Tell me about yourself, your family, or any god damn thing on this earth.'

It's true – your whole life flashes in front of your eyes when you are about to die. My life was flashing before my eyes, still trying to identify the real Vijay... 'Vijay' as my Grandpa used to tell me: 'The Victorious One'.

'Doc, I'll tell you a story, my story. This story is about a mountain, a little stream and fire. I am Vijay Amrit Raj Sharma. Sorry, I'm not a civilian – Captain Vijay Amrit Raj Sharma, son of Suhasani and Jaganath Sharma, for the past four years, commissioned in the twelfth battalion, The Rajputana Rifles, today struggling between life and death...

One

Aum
Bhur Bhuvah Swaha
Tat Savitur Varenyam
Bhargo Devasya Dheemahi
Dhiyo Yo Nah Prachodayat

"O Divine Mother, our hearts are filled with darkness. Please make this darkness distant from us and illuminate us from within."

These were the first words that I would hear every morning, as my grandfather, Pandit Bhuvnesh Sharma would recite the *Gayatri Mantra* after his morning prayers, ready to go to the temple. Life is your biggest teacher; its lessons remain with you forever. It teaches you virtues, struggles, and the most important lesson, faith; faith in yourself, in others and in God. Jaganath Sharma, my father, never taught me anything; he died when I was seven. The day I was born, people mourned. I was born with my mother's blood smeared all over my body; she died due to excessive bleeding while giving birth to me. After that, my father was a shattered man who died due to excessive alcohol intake that led to liver cirrhosis. I don't know whether my father's sorrow dissolved in a wine glass because of his love for my mother or it was an excuse for his weakness. And so, whatever I am today, it is all because of my grandfather, Pandit Bhuvnesh Sharma.

"Failure is not a crime. Failure to learn from failure is." **During** our school days, we were taught a lesson and then a test was given. However, life teaches you the other way around. It gives you the test first and then teaches you the lesson. I've always been a good learner, but only learning the way life teaches. There have been many intellectuals, philosophers, scientists and historians to teach you about the greatest lessons of life; I am none of them, but I do have a few lessons to share with you that life has managed to teach me.

Childhood memories are bleak; they are like a mirror covered with mist. Something is there but not clearly seen. My memories of childhood are not crystal clear except for a few things that I remember distinctly. My grandfather's morning chants of the *Gayatri mantra*, a few murmurs in the neighborhood about the death of my mother and later the death of my father. It was thirty years ago when my grandfather moved to Mussoorie, a small hill station in the northern part of India from our native village somewhere in the interiors of Garhwal hills. One of our distant relatives helped my grandfather by getting him appointed as the temple priest. Apart from this, he was lucky to get accommodation in the outhouse of Kumar Villa. He was the caretaker of Kumars' property and was paid two thousand rupees apart from free lodging in their outhouse. The Kumars came only for a couple of months, during the summer. The main entrance of Kumar Villa had a pair of huge iron gates, which opened only when the Kumars were there. In the backyard, there was a small opening which was the entrance to the outhouse. The outhouse had a huge room, with a veranda overlooking the Kumar Villa. It had a separate storeroom and a bathroom outside the house. It had a single room with a double bed in one corner, while the other corner had a wooden table, which was used for studies and as a makeshift dressing table. There was only one entrance through the kitchen into the single large room leading to the veranda. It was shabby, dimly lit by a single bulb dangling down with an electric wire from the roof.

Hampton Court was my first school. My Grandfather believed that education is the key to success in all spheres of life. And so, despite being a poor temple priest, he ensured that I was educated in one of the best schools in Mussoorie. I remember, my classroom had colorful paintings of Mickey and Donald on its rear wall. I also remember my class-teacher, Miss Anita, and the strong perfume she wore with her colorful outfit; that fragrance is still embedded somewhere deep inside my memories. There was a girl, Nikita, who had green eyes; I always used to wonder, why she had green eyes. I know those were the most beautiful eyes in the world. Sumit, the chubby boy, Seth Aggarwal's son, shared the bench with me. Sumit's dad was one of the leading businessmen of Mussoorie. Sumit had all the fancy, bright and expensive stuff. His clothes, toys, stationery and lunch-box always were the best in class.

I've always had a great fascination for pens, especially the fountain pen. Sumit had a Chinese fountain pen. It was bright red in color, with a golden nib. I had developed a weakness for that pen. Every day, I used to take that pen from him to play with and would wish that I could own a similar pen. Then one day, I saw that pen lying under my desk; it might have fallen down and Sumit was unaware. My initial intention was to pick it up and return it to Sumit, but then I was tempted to keep it in my bag; no one would come to know if I hid it. I know now that it was not the right thing to do, but at the age of six, you lack the power to differentiate between what is right and what is wrong. My desire for the pen had tempted me to do something, which made me nervous and afraid for the first time in my life. I quietly went under the desk, picked up the pen and dropped it in my bag. I don't know whether I was happy or uncomfortable but I knew the pen was mine from now.

The next morning my grandfather saw the pen in my bag while he was placing the tiffin-box in my bag. He asked me about the pen. I never lied to my grandfather. Moreover, I had absolute faith in him, and so I told him exactly what had happened. My grandfather heard every word carefully. I looked at him and tears ran down my face. I knew I had done something wrong and I was now ashamed to face my grandfather.

'Vijay, listen carefully to what I tell you today.' My grandfather sat me in his lap and said these words, looking straight into my eyes. I could barely look at him, but his words are still with me.

'This lesson must always remain with you forever. You must know what is necessary. You must be wise enough as you grow, to know the difference between what is right and what is wrong. The important thing is not the pen but the act behind getting the pen, which is called stealing. We are all subject to deception and often get carried away with temptation but you must learn to differentiate between what is right and what is wrong. This pen may not be important for you or to the one whom you have stolen it from, but your actions are important, which will dictate your life and what you will become in the future.'

I might not have learned any lesson that day if that pen was not discovered by my grandfather. Sumit himself was not aware that he had lost that pen. He only realised when I returned the pen to him. I still thank my stars that the pen was discovered by my grandfather before I could hide it, else I might have been tempted to steal other things, which might have continued from there on. The first lesson my grandfather and life taught me has always remained with me. Loss of the ability to differentiate is the greatest source of danger. One must have the wisdom to judge what is right and wrong. The right path may not be the best suited, but it will definitely be the best one.

I grew up in the shade of the apple trees of the Kumar villa orchard, learning how to nurture the flowers with the gardener, Santu. I grew up with temple chants, performing the sacred ablutions. Grandpa educated me in his own way, the way he had learned from his father. Every evening, he would tell me stories from Indian mythology about Lord Rama, Lord Krishna, tales from Ramayana and the Mahabharata. He told me that learning is a continuous process and everything that is present in this universe teaches you a lesson.

'A student should always imbibe these qualities in him', Grandpa would say and recite a few lines in Sanskrit giving various qualities of animals. 'Be like a crow, it always shares, never eats alone. Whenever a crow finds a piece of bread, it cries out loud inviting others to join. Be like a rooster, for when it fights it puts in all his strength. Be like a dog, always alert. Even if a dog is asleep, the slightest of sounds is enough to wake him up. Be like a crane, and watch how it concentrates when it catches a fish and lastly, the most important of all, be like an ant, it may fall again and again while climbing a hill but it never gives up.'

Grandpa taught me that everything is divine and the reason we pray to everything. The birds, animals, nature, rivers, everything is a form of God. Often, I used to ask grandpa the same question again and again:

'What does God mean?'

'Everything that you see is divine, it is God', Grandpa would reply, indicating the sky, the mountains and the earth.

'Am I also God, grandpa?'

'Yes you are, my angel.' Grandpa would smile and kiss my forehead.

'Where do we go after we die?'

'We become a star.'

'Can we see momma?'

'Yes', Grandpa would nod his head.

'If I ask something from God, will he listen to me?'

'God listens and fulfills your wish if your prayer is strong enough to reach God's ears', Grandpa told me. 'Whenever you desire, desire for the right thing, because you never know what you wish for may come true.' I always used to wonder if at all it could be true. But I never asked anything from God but always believed in His supremacy. I believed that there is some force running this universe, unseen and unheard of, yet we can feel its presence.

Although I have always been an average student, grandpa always encouraged me to do well in studies. He recited a verse in Sanskrit often. I don't remember the exact words, but I know what it meant.

A lazy person will not gain knowledge.
If you are not wise, you will not earn money.
If you are poor, you will not have friends.
And there is no happiness without friends.

Life is a wheel, always turning with events good and bad, with hope and despair and in the shades of joys and sorrows. Grandpa told me to never loose your head when you taste the sweet fruit of success, just thank God that he has been kind to you. Whenever I was in distress, Grandpa always told me:

Tu to dariya hai apni manzil dhoond hi lega,
Rastae to karwan ko chaiyae.
Tu behta ja ganga ki tarah.

You are like a flowing river that will make its own way.
The roads are for the others.
Keep moving ahead like a flowing river. The path is the way.

Occasionally, we went to Dehradun, at Forest Research Institute (FRI), where my grandfather's younger brother lived with his three sons and their children. He worked there as a lower division clerk. I remember the game of hide-and-seek we played in the litchi orchard. We often heard scary stories from our uncle about the witch who lived in the litchi orchard. The frightful witch was fond of trapping little children for her dinner soup. After dark, the litchi orchard was the scariest place and till date, the unknown witch haunts me in my nightmares.

Days passed by, night after night, months after months and year after year. I grew up and the only relationship I understood was my grandfather. He was my mother, he was my father, my mentor, my guide and my friend. But after my intermediate, I was about to discover something very special, I know I was late yet some relationships do touch you at some stage of life. Love and friendship are two such forms of relationships and they were about to touch my life in Municipal Post Graduate College of Mussoorie. What these two forms of relationships have taught me, I know, is the essence of life, it's the universal law of physics – The Law of Gravity; attraction. It is proved that gravity dictates the equilibrium of all heavenly bodies and it is also prevalent in the stability of the elementary form of matter. This gravity was about to dictate my life. The year was 1994, the year without mobile phones, without reality shows and without the Internet...

Two

It was another summer evening. Philip Thomas adjusted his guitar strings and checked the tune to his perfection. Then he removed a red plectrum from his jeans' coin pocket and struck the guitar to catch the attention of the guests. Until now, none of the customers had noticed him, but with the musical chords arresting the ambiance, there was silence for a while in the bar. All eyes were focused on the guitar player. Philip adjusted the tension on a couple of strings, and then strummed again. This time, the sound was perfect.

'Good evening, ladies and gentlemen. This is Philip Thomas, the guitar player and I will be entertaining you for the evening. After the first song, you may send in your requests.'

Philip started the evening, as usual, with his favorite song, "*Stairway to Heaven*". It was a ritual, a hymn for him to start the evening with this song. This song was special to him, close to his heart; it was the first song he had learnt how to play on the guitar. The show had now begun and requests were flooding in from all corners of the bar. One song after the other and all were spellbound; an evening to remember for all the guests. A few thought that they were lucky to get a table, because after nine it was nearly impossible to get one.

It was past midnight, but requests were still pouring in for more songs: 'My boy, you are brilliant! One last number, come on, let's have some Beatles!' shouted an old gentleman from the corner table.

'One last Dire Straits!' someone shouted in the middle. 'Simon and Garfunkel!', 'Let's have a Sufi number!', 'A love song', 'Hindi melody!' People were crazy, and at times, it was difficult to handle them. As per the contract, Philip was to entertain guests from 8pm to 11pm but often he overshot. Were people crazy or was there magic in Philip's guitar?

Philip quickly unplugged the jack and started closing for the day. 'Sorry friends, no more request for the day, the show will continue tomorrow.'

Philip was like the mountains, steady, strong, and quite solid. At times, he appeared blue, like the shadows across the mountains when the sun is across the horizon, deep in his own thoughts, trying to discover his identity. At times, he was like the Himalayas, covered with white snow, a reflection of purity and at the same time how easily it could catch dirt. At times, he was like an underground volcano, ready to explode, the monster in him portraying hatred against everyone, complaining about his identity.

Philip was an orphan, no one knew about his parents. About twenty years ago, Father Thomas had found a newborn baby crying for his mother at the church doorstep. Probably, he was an unwanted child and no one was willing to welcome him into this world. Father Thomas tried to inquire about his parents but when he got no clue, he decided to be his legal guardian. Philip grew up with the Patricians Brothers and Sisters and was sent to their missionary school from where he did his intermediate. After schooling, he was doing his graduation from Municipal Post Graduate College and that's where we became friends.

Philip was a member of the carol masses in church; he played guitar and sang hymns every Sunday. Philip wanted to pursue music as his career. He wanted to compose music, but a career like that rarely pays good dividends. The best the world could offer him was a part-time job at Tavern bar. During peak seasons, he earned ten thousand rupees a month. During off-seasons, he gave guitar lessons to school children.

Radha woke up with the first sunlight. Her face fresh as the morning dew on the petals, her hair scattered like the autumn clouds and her eyes shimmering with a thousand dreams.

Radha plaited her waist length hair and tied it with a colorful band, a touch of lipstick on her lips and then carefully applied *kajal* on her shimmering eyes. She carefully inspected herself in the mirror. She smiled at herself and moved towards the college.

Radha was like the stream flowing gently on the curves of the mountains, finding a way out towards the ocean. She wanted to run away but yet she was attached to these mountains. Water cannot give you support, but life and hope appears in its form. Radha was life, she was hope and she was love.

Philip was waiting for me on his Enfield motorbike. Philip had earned enough at the Tavern bar and the guitar tuitions to buy himself a second-hand Enfield Bullet.

'Vijay, today again you are late', Philip said, removing his aviators and looking at me with a frown.

'I'm sorry, Philip', I looked at him apologetically; Philip was pleased whenever anyone apologised. Girls were crazy for Philip – he was perfect in all aspects: tall, dark and handsome. On top of that, he had a well-maintained Enfield Bullet, a pair of Ray-Ban aviator shades gifted by one of the tourists at the Tavern bar, amazing guitar-playing skills and a melodious voice.

I sat behind him and held him tightly; the motorbike gave a solid jerk as it moved ahead. We started rolling downhill towards the college. Philip switched off the ignition and the bike moved with the gravity, a common feature in the hills to save fuel.

'Where are we going?' I asked, witnessing the college gate pass while we kept rolling down.

'We are going to Dehradun.'

'But why?' I asked.

'I have to buy something. Don't worry, I will also take you for a movie.' Who wanted to waste time on movies, but then refusing Philip was difficult; friends are by choice and not by default. On any given day, Philip would do anything for me and I was aware of the fact. That was what our friendship was all about.

We didn't stop until we reached Dehradun. Philip stopped in front of a big showroom, the most expensive showroom in the city.

'What do you want to buy? We could have bought it from Mussoorie', I said, swinging my leg to get down from the bike.

'Good things are not available in Mussoorie.'

'What is so special that we have come all the way to Dehradun?' I asked, looking a bit annoyed.

'Have patience, buddy, I know you will make up for today's loss', Philip said, putting the bike on stand.

'Select a watch that you think is good.'

I kept staring at Philip unable to decipher what was going on. I was confused.

'Why?'

'I need to buy a watch for someone.' After a little looking around, I spotted a watch that was sleek and sporty.

'How much does this watch cost?' I asked the shopkeeper.

'This is a Swiss watch; it has a lifetime guarantee and costs only six thousand rupees.' Six thousand was too much for students like us.

'Could you show us more with a similar pattern but a little less on the price?' I asked the shopkeeper, but Philip held me back.

'No, no- we will buy this one.' Philip paid the bill and got the watch neatly gift wrapped.

After shopping, we went for a matinée show; Philip insisted a lot. It was a useless Hindi movie. The hero was an illiterate, unemployed youth who flexed his muscles in front of all bad guys. He fell in love with a rich girl who had nothing to do other than wear provocative clothes and dance with the hero. The girl's dad was a millionaire but also a crook involved in all sorts of illegal activities. Finally, the girl eloped with the hero, the girl's dad chased them and that continued, till the end. At the end, the hero killed all the bad guys and wins her father's blessing.

After a good meal of momos and chicken soup at a roadside vendor, we started back towards Mussoorie. It was the first week of November and the wind was uncomfortably cold. It had moisture in it; we could sense that there had been a spell of rain in the upper reaches. As we moved uphill, it started raining. I was hiding behind Philip's broad body frame, protecting myself from the cold wind, while Philip was humming the song "*November Rain*" by Guns n Roses.

Towards the valley, the sun was crossing the horizon, smearing red all over the sky. In the opposite direction, towards the hills, one could hear the thunder roar and lightening. In the mountains, the rains come down with retribution. In no time, the rain grew heavy and turned into a hailstorm, we had barely reached midway; a place called Chunakhala. It was impossible to move ahead. We spotted a small shop and decided to take a break until the hailstorm stopped.

The shop was closed but the dim light of a hurricane lamp convinced us that there was someone inside. I pushed the door; it was open. We hurried inside, dripping from head to toe. An old man was sitting close to the fire with his knees drawn to his chest. He seemed like a man with a tempest in him. In the dim light too, his face reflected many untold stories of a sad, oppressive silence in his wrinkled face.

'It's raining heavily', Philip said to attract his attention, but because of the noise of the hail falling on the corrugated roof, the old man was unable to hear. Philip repeated the sentence, this time at a higher pitch and the old man noticed. He startled and looked towards the door.

'You guys scared me', he said.

'We are sorry but we had no other shelter', Philip said

'You people are also stuck like me', said the old man. 'Where are you guys heading to?' He almost shouted.

'We were going towards Mussoorie, but got stuck here. We will have to wait until the hailstorm mellows down', Philip said, sitting close to the fire, trying to dry his clothes.

'This is cold November rain, it will continue for some time. I think we all might have to stay here for the night.' The old man wagged his hand indicating me to come close to the fire. I was busy wiping off drops of water from my face.

'Would you like to have something?' The old man was glad to see customers visiting him even after dark. Thanks to the heavens above.

'Tea and bun omelettes for us', Philip ordered. I was amazed; Philip was still feeling hungry after three plates of momos and two chicken soups. He could eat anything, anytime and anywhere.

The old man got busy preparing the tea and omelette. 'Where do you stay?' Philip asked the old man who was carefully chopping onions with a sharp-edged knife.

'I stay nearby, just a 10-minute walk from here', the old man said, putting a few dried twigs into the fire.

'Vijay, this rain will not stop till morning, we are stuck here. Your grandpa will worry for you', Philip said, looking towards me; I acknowledged his concern by nodding my head.

Hot sweet tea and a burger made of spicy omelettes was as good as any scrumptious meal at a five star hotel. After a good delicacy at the tea stall and waiting patiently for three hours, we realised that the rain will not stop and it was too late to travel on forlorn mountain roads. We decided to stay with the old man for the night. The old man gave us a jute mat and a blanket to share. I shifted the wooden benches placed for customers to one side while Philip unrolled the mat on the mud-smeared floor. By that time our clothes had dried up. Both of us slid inside the blanket, shivering and pulling the blanket towards our end.

Philip was lost in his own world thinking something. I turned my back to Philip and closed my eyes. It was still raining outside. The music of raindrops falling on the corrugated roof was intoxicating. In no time, I was fast asleep.

I opened my eyes; soft music was melting in my ears. Philip was awake, playing his harmonica. The rain had mellowed down to a drizzle; it was still dark outside. Philip was shivering; I thought I had pulled the blanket towards my side and that was the reason why Philip was shivering but then I realised his palm was hot like a burning stove. I placed my hand on his forehead; Philip's body temperature was high.

'Philip, you are down with a fever', I said.

'I think it's because of the cold wind and the rain. Don't worry, I will be alright.' The rain had stopped by now. We were lying facing each other inside the blanket.

'I love my mother', Philip said. His words took me by surprise. Mother; it was a familiar word for both of us, yet we never knew what it meant.

'I don't know who she was and why she abandoned me but I feel society is more to be blamed than my mother. And the biggest culprit is my dad who did not have the guts to hold my mother's hand', Philip said, shivering inside the blanket.

'Society is a curse on mankind. They are not to protect the oppressed and the weak but they lick the strong and the powerful. Love has disappeared from this earth and only thing that is left behind is lust with its remnants in my shape.' I had never seen Philip so disturbed. This was the first time I had seen him so sentimental and dismayed.

'Don't stress your mind, go off to sleep', I said, turning my back to him, pretending to sleep. I tried to close my eyes and sleep but it was difficult to sleep again. The sky was clearing up; the moon was peeping inside the shop from the small window over our heads. Philip was still awake, playing a soft, sad tune on his harmonica. I turned around to face him; the moonlight was lighting his oval face and Philip's eyes were shining in the dark. Philip was playing a melancholy tune, admiring the darkness, lost in his own world.

'Philip, what are you thinking?' I asked, curling my arm under my head.

'Nothing', Philip gently turned his face towards me. I wiped the little droplets of sweat from his forehead.

'You should try to sleep. Don't think about useless things in life.' I turned my back again, pretending to sleep. Philip continued to admire the darkness and played the same melancholy tune on his harmonica.

I couldn't sleep either and kept staring at the full moon shining outside from the broken window. I recalled what grandpa told me once, he told me that the biggest thing we all are seeking is recognition; an identity for the world to know you. Grandpa gave me examples from the two great epic tales of *Mahabharata* and *Ramayana*.

In the epic tale of *Ramayana*, Lord Rama was destined to become the king of Ayodhya and yet, circumstances forced him to live in exile for fourteen years. The greater reason being that Lord Rama had to identify himself and more important was the triumph of good over evil, which made him an accepted king by the people of Ayodhya. Similarly, in the epic tale of Mahabharata, we witness a bloody battle between the Kauravas and the Pandavas who were brothers. It may appear on the surface as a battle to acquire the kingdom which could have been divided equally, but if we view it deeply, it was a battle of recognition. Today, the same question was in Philip's eyes. He wanted his identity, his solitude was screaming out to ask the world his name, a name, which the world must recognize at any cost. Yes, I understood the importance of a name; the name, the identity, the recognition.

The first light brought a new ray of hope indicating clear sky along with the chirping of birds, and we headed towards Mussoorie.

Three

That day, we were before time, and this was the first time in three years that we were early. Philip was still down with a fever but had opted to come to college. Then, a little smile ran through my face as Philip indicated something at the college gate. It was Radha entering with a notebook in her hand, dressed in a bright red *salwar kameez*. Radha was also our best friend in college.

Radha was walking towards me. She was lovely and elegant. Again, the same law of gravity was prevalent, beauty attracts everyone and first time this gravity was pulling me mercilessly towards itself.

'Happy birthday, Vijay!' she wished me as soon as she approached. I was a bit surprised; I never expected others to remember my birthday, especially Radha.

Philip took out the watch we had purchased and handed it to me. 'Happy Birthday, Vijay! This is for you, from me and Radha.'

I gave him a bewildered look, unable to believe it. 'It's unfair, Philip, you cannot waste so much money on me.'

'Don't worry, Radha has contributed two thousand,' Philip said.

'That's not done, really not done.' I took the watch from Philip's hand my voice trembling with joy and anguish; joy not because of the present, but because of friends like Philip and Radha. Anguish, because I was unable to reciprocate.

'I'll get something for you guys', I was choking, as I rushed towards the canteen, quickly wiping tears from the edge of my eyes. I came back with a few packets of chips, patties, three bottles of coke and a couple of pastries joined together with a mini candle placed on top of it. We used a spoon to cut the modified cake. After our treat, we realised it was time for our classes.

'Ten-thirty, time for classes', Radha said with a smile.

'I think we should revise the important questions marked in your notebook. No point wasting our time in useless classes.' I knew exams were nearing and we must get some momentum to pass. Philip and I never wasted time in preparing notes but studied from Radha's notes. Radha was very particular about preparing notes and she had a good handwriting, which was an asset for us. She also marked all the important questions, which were read over by her every day in the college, sitting beside the pond on the grass lawn.

Radha started reading the important questions while Philip lay in the pleasant sunshine with his head resting on my lap. Philip was absently plucking blades of grass from the lawn. The sun sparkled in the pond with little colorful fishes dancing in it. Philip closed his eyes and was soon fast asleep in the warmth of the sunshine.

Today, I was not listening to what was being revised but I was admiring Radha's beautiful face. Was she looking more magnetic today or was it that I was looking at her carefully for the first time? I had been engrossed in my own world, the reason why I never realised that she was pretty, and indeed her beauty was her simplicity. Her fair complexion and the little secret of her sweetness was the solitary dimple on the edge of her left cheek. Her eyes had a promise of hope and her voice melodious. Something was charismatic about her.

I kept thinking about her. Radha, how lyrical her name sounded, like poetry; her shimmering eyes had so many untold stories, and her countenance was an epic in itself. Radha, only one thing on my mind.

Your magical eyes tell me a story
Your voice hums like a melody
Oh, Radha, how come I haven't noticed you for so long?

I was noting down something else today: Radha, one word to say it all. *Love seeks no cause beyond itself and no fruit; it is its own fruit, its own enjoyment.*

The sun was setting behind the hills and something was rising in my heart: Radha.

Tavern bar is one of the most happening places in Mussoorie; especially during peak season. If you happen to visit Mussoorie, never miss it or you may repent later. It is special because of three things: first, excellent food; second, a bar serving various kinds of poisons and above all, for Philip, the guitar player.

Again it was midnight and requests were still pouring in for one more song. 'My boy, I bet you will be a star one day!' shouted an old gentleman from one of the tables.

'One last song for my wife, please, my dear boy!' someone shouted from the center table. '"*Lady in Red*"!'

'Pink Floyd!' shouted a hippie-looking teenager, making rings of smoke from the corner table.

'Let's have a Nusrat *sahib*'s Sufi number, a love song Hindi melody.'

'Sorry friends, no more requests for the day, the show will continue tomorrow', Philip said, as usual.

'Would you play one last request for me?' A girl dressed in an emerald top and blue jeans approached Philip, who was busy packing his instruments. She had a friendly face with a soft smile.

'Sorry, Ma'am, I've already overshot my timings for the day.'

'All right, here is my request. Tomorrow I hope you start the show with my request.' She handed a neatly folded paper-napkin with a note written on it, to him.

Request from Sonia, for the song "I just called to say I love you".

There was a 500-rupee bill neatly attached with it. Philip folded the paper and kept it in his pocket.

'I promise you, ma'am, tomorrow the show will begin with your request, and I want you to occupy the seat right in front of me.' Philip placed the guitar inside the case and without wasting much time, went out.

The next evening, Sonia entered the restaurant sharp at 7.30pm. Philip came at 8pm, saw Sonia occupying the front seat, and an immense wave of joy ran through his face. He smiled at her and Sonia responded with a soft smile acknowledging him. Philip looked at Sonia carefully, she was definitely beautiful. Without wasting much time, he got ready for the show. He placed the attachment to his acoustic guitar and pulling out the plectrum from his jeans' coin pocket he was ready for the show.

'Ladies and gentlemen, today's request begins with a love song. The request comes from a beautiful lady sitting right in front of me, Sonia.' This was the first time the custom was broken and the show did not begin with "*Stairway to Heaven*".

Philip started humming and people were captivated by his melodious voice. Sonia watched him carefully; she was in a different world, someone in her thoughts. Was it Philip?

Later, Philip returned the same napkin with the five hundred-rupee note back to Sonia The back side of the paper-napkin had his reply:

Money is not the sole purpose that I sing for. It's my passion – Philip.

That evening Philip received a call from Sonia.

'Hi Philip, this is Sonia.'

'Hello, ma'am, I'm really surprised to receive your call.'

'Don't be surprised, I just called to say that you have a great voice.'

'Thanks ma'am, appreciation is the only thing that an artist looks forward to.'

'You have returned the money; I was feeling bad so I decided to call you. I would like to reciprocate. How about having dinner with me tomorrow?' Sonia asked.

'That is absolutely not required.'

'But I insist, I really want to take you out for dinner.'

'Ma'am, dinner would be difficult since I'm committed, but I think lunch would be OK.'

'Then shall we meet at Tavern, 1pm.'

'No, ma'am, not Tavern. I would be uncomfortable over there since I'm their employee. There is another place, "Momo's". I hope you like Tibetan and Chinese food?'

'Done. I'll wait for you at picture palace, sharp at 12:30pm. One more thing, don't call me "ma'am". It sounds I'm old and dull. Everyone prefers to hear their name. Call me "Sonia".' The call was disconnected. Philip couldn't help smiling at himself.

I went to meet Philip; normally on Sundays we have lunch together and discussed important questions. I went to the missionary's church where Philip stayed but I was unable to find him. Disheartened and dejected I was heading back towards home, this was the first time Philip was away and I never got a hint where he was. As I was moving back, I met Father Thomas.

'Good afternoon, Father', I greeted the old father with a friendly smile.

'God bless you, my child, but how come you are here? Where is your friend?' Father asked.

'I don't know, Father; I am looking for him.'

'But he told me he is going out and will have lunch outside; I never knew you were not with him. Is there anything important? Let me know, I will inform him.'

'Actually, Father, last night I completed the story I was writing, I wanted him to read it and give me his comments', I said, showing the diary to Father Thomas.

'That's wonderful, my child! So we have a budding writer in you.'

'Would you like to read my story?' I asked.

'Definitely, my child. Let me see what you have to offer to this world.' Father Thomas took the notebook from my hand and went inside the church.

Four

'Hey Vijay, I forgot, Father Thomas had given this notebook of yours to me. I never got the chance to read your story but he praised it a lot.' He handed me my diary.

I opened it and there was a note written by Father Thomas:

Dear Vijay,

God bless you, my child. I have gone through your story and found it gripping right from the word 'go'. I pray to God for your success and I can see a writer in you who would definitely contribute to the world some substance. It is very much required; the world is full of unread trash.

One thing I would like to add: Always remember it's never too late for a good deed, killing is not the solution to a problem.

Looking forward for your next story.

Radha took the notebook from my hand and started reading the note written by Father Thomas. 'What's the story about?' she asked, inspecting the notebook.

'The story is about an Army officer who decides to quit after he gets his second gallantry award', I said.

'But why?' asked Radha.

'Because he kills his friend.'

'It doesn't sound convincing; friendship is meant to die for each other and not kill', Radha said, brusquely.

'Read the story, there is something more to it.'

'I'll read it for sure.'

I was sulking, the reason was Philip's absence yesterday and Philip got a hint about it.

'Yesterday, I was on a date', Philip said.

'You were on a date! Are you kidding? With whom? Where?' I said with startled exclamation.

'Sonia. Her name is Sonia; she's one of the tourists.' Philip said with patronizing grin.

'Never trust these tourists; they just look forward to having a good time here', Radha said, strictly.

'Come on champ, you are great! Tell me, when do we get to meet her?' I was excited as if a child had just discovered a bunch of chocolates under his pillow.

'I'm planning for a picnic tomorrow and you all are cordially invited, but remember guys, we will go early, we will walk up to the stream.'

'I don't have time for all this', Radha admonished. 'There are other important household chores to be finished on a Sunday.'

'Come on, don't be a spoilsport. It will be fun', I said, pulling Radha by her sleeves.

'Get some lunch wrapped up. I'll get some beer', Philip said.

'We don't drink', I said.

'Fruit juice for non drinkers', Philip got up. 'Sharp at eight in the morning, reach Lal Tibba. I'll get Sonia along with me.'

It was the day of the picnic and Philip was wearing his faded denim jeans and his favorite white T-shirt. Sonia was in a comfortable Capri and loose yellow top, sporting a hat. I, as usual, was simply turned out in gray trousers and a plain shirt. Radha looked pretty in her ivory *salwar kameez* with a hint of peacock green shades. She had a neatly knotted ponytail hanging to her waist. The food and beer bottles were in a bag slung on my shoulder, while Philip slung his guitar across his back.

Philip introduced Sonia to Radha and me. I greeted her with a friendly handshake and winked at Philip. Radha never said anything but started adjusting her hair to pretend to look busy.

'Everybody in?' said Philip. 'If so, let's move.'

The sun was rising languidly over the hills, peeping between wandering clouds. It was a two hour-walk to the river, only if Sonia could keep up the pace with others.

The thick deodar trees were hiding the river; it was there, the giggling confirmed it, but it was not visible. The mountain ridge seemed unending and they had to walk on the steep slope. Sonia was a bit uncomfortable walking on slippery grass and stony path.

'How far is it? I'm tired', Sonia said, pulling Philip's arm. I gave a teasing smile to Radha who scowled at Sonia with mocking face.

'We are already here', Philip said holding her hand.

I again smiled at Radha, who wrinkled her nose at Philip and Sonia and said,

'We highlanders can walk miles, we are used to walking long distances but people from plains lack stamina.'

The path to the river became steeper towards the valley and Sonia was almost clinging to Philip for support. This route was mostly used by villagers, shepherds and a few milkmen; it was a woozy, winding path. Radha slipped, and witnessing Radha plummet, Sonia giggled and her giggle had a mocking tune. Radha gave her a grotesque look; I stretched my hand to pull her up.

Soon we were in the valley and the path straightened. A group of green parrots screeched and flew above us. After crossing a few boulders and little rivulet, we reached the river. The water in the river was hastening and jumping with joy, moving on to find a new world.

We reached a little knoll where we decided to camp. Right in front was a little waterfall, the falling water fashioned a static pond for the fishes to dance in the shimmering sun. Radha unrolled the bed sheet on the grass, I spread out the eatables while Philip carefully kept his guitar against a boulder and quickly placed the beer bottles inside the icy cool river water.

'Oh God, I'm tired', Sonia said, lying down on the grass.

'People from the plains are quite weak. Coming down is easy; don't forget we have to climb all the way up', Radha scoffed.

'Don't worry, Philip is there to take care of me, he will drag me along with him', Sonia replied abruptly. Philip and I could sense the uneasiness in the air.

There was plenty of water in the river, clear like mirror with silver fishes dancing in it.

'It is not very deep', said Philip, folding his jeans up to his thighs. He stretched out his hand and assisted Sonia into the cool running water.

I followed, while Radha looked at them still sulking.

'Water is not very cold, why you don't come in?' I said to Radha.

'I'm fine, you people enjoy. As it is you have great company, you don't need me', Radha said, brusquely.

After a few moments of water slapping at each other, we decided to join Radha at the knoll.

'Radha, come let's eat something', I said, to get some easiness.

After silence for some time, I decided to break the ice, 'Philip, let's have a song from you. Sonia, the request should be from your side.'

'He is good at all numbers, any soft rock would do', replied Sonia sedately.

Philip picked his guitar up and looked at Radha, she was sulking. Philip knew his closeness with Sonia was the reason.

'OK, Sonia I'll play a Sufi number, Radha's favorite.' Radha looked at Philip with raised eyebrows on hearing her name.

'Radha, do you remember the song?' Philip asked

'No, I don't. You can play a hip-hop English number.' Radha was still sulking.

'Come on, Radha, the one I played on your birthday?' Philip was still trying hard to make her comfortable. To add fuel to fire, Sonia adjusted herself closer to Philip.

'OK, this is Radha's favorite song, a Sufi number called "*Tere Ishq Mein*".'

Intentionally, Philip started the song with Radha's favorite verse, plucking his guitar. Radha smiled and looked at him. Philip knew it was working. The song continued.

The song was beautiful and Philip's voice had magic in it. The spell worked and a wide smile ran across Radha's face.

'Hey Vijay, I forgot to tell you, I have completed your story', Radha said.

'So what do you feel about it?' I asked, resting my back against the boulder.

'To be true I liked it, it was indeed gripping, but ending could have been a little different.'

'Are you a writer?' Sonia asked me.

'No... no nothing serious, it was just a stupid story in my mind and I gave it a try', I said, adjusting my hands to comfort my head.

'What's the story?' Sonia asked Radha, it looked like the cold war between them was coming to an end.

'The story is about two friends', Radha said pursing her lips. 'One becomes an Army officer while the other is forced into illegal activities. The security forces mark him a terrorist, but he is innocent. The ending is sad because the protagonist kills his own friend.'

'Sounds interesting', remarked Sonia.

'I feel the protagonist should have gone out of his way to save his friend that would have been better', Radha said.

'One of my friends is an editor at a newspaper; you give me your script and I would try to get it published in one of the newspapers.'

My eyes sparkled, 'I hope you are serious?' I said, enthusiastically.

'I can only try; rest depends on the story and your luck', Sonia said, shrugging her shoulders.

'I can assure you, the story is good', Radha said confidently, somehow she had faith in my talent.

'That's great, cheers to this!' Raising a toast in my name, Philip opened a beer bottle and handed it to Sonia.

The sun moved over the river and across the branches of the trees. Soon we realised we must start climbing uphill before it gets dark. I packed the leftover stuff, while Philip carefully packed his guitar and we started moving up. We were perspiring copiously by the time we reached the hilltop. Sonia was being dragged by Philip and was dead by the time she reached uphill. The sun had shifted behind the hill.

We started moving at a slow pace towards picture palace. At picture palace we noticed a few of our colleagues sitting at a tea-shop. A few empty tea glasses were lying on the table. A few were sipping their tea while some were smoking. Their faces were tensed and morose. All seemed to be engaged in some serious discussion between them.

Philip noticed it was Ballu, the college president and a few other elected members. We wanted to avoid them else rumors would monger that we were out with girls. Mussoorie is a small place and everyone is a familiar face apart from the tourists.

'Hey Philip!' Ballu shouted, we were unable to escape from Ballu's eyes. Philip told me to stay there with the girls while he went to meet Ballu.

'Hi brother, what's up?' Philip asked.

'Did you hear the news?' Ballu asked, making a ring of smoke in the air.

'What happened?' Philip asked.

'Twelve of our people have been shot dead by the police on their way to Delhi', Ballu said, looking anxious. For quite some time, agitation was going on; the hill people wanted a hill state for them. They had moved in buses to Delhi, planning for a peaceful protest at the parliament.

'But why? It was supposed to be a peaceful protest', Philip asked.

'The bus was stopped near Muzaffarnagar, the crowd got agitated and in return, police opened fire. A few of our women were also raped by a few notorious policemen.'

'Oh my God! What is happening? What about the twelve who died?' Philip asked, his facial expression changing on hearing the news.

'I don't know the toll may increase. My elder brother was one of those who got killed', Ballu said and burst into tears.

Sunil came and comforted Ballu. Sunil was the general secretary; his father was a prominent political figure in Mussoorie.

'Don't worry, brother, we will not keep silent, this fire will now go a long way. We will continue to fight for our rights. The sacrifice made by our brothers and sisters cannot go in vain. We are willing to die, all are united', Sunil said. 'Philip, just spread a word that there will be a students' meeting in the college campus tomorrow, at nine.'

'Surely brother, I will', Philip said.

'We need your support, Philip. In difficult times we need to stand by each other', Sunil clasped his hand against Philip's shoulder.

Philip went back and informed me about the incident. 'I think we should stay out of this', I said.

'I really don't know but I'm feeling a bit disturbed about whatever has happened.'

For about a week, the agitation was going on and things seemed to be quite peaceful, but now the authorities had decided to come cracking on the protesters. The news had spread like wildfire and one could see tourists packing and moving out by whatever was available – private vehicles, hired cabs, buses, they were all rolling downhill.

'Sonia, I think you should move out tonight, things might go out of hand and you might get stuck out here', Philip said, looking towards Sonia, his eyes portraying fear and uncertainty.

'There are three more girls who have come with me', Sonia said, looking sheepishly towards Philip. Radha held her shoulder, consoling her.

'You rush to your hotel and pack your stuff. In the mean time, I will get a cab arranged for you.'

The rest of the time it was silence, vagueness on our minds. These kind of incidents may be common for rest of the world, but for Mussoorie it was a new occurrence altogether. It was frightening news, a time to hold each other's hand. I could sense it but fear was overpowering me. Philip knew he had to stand by his fellowmen; if not in good times he would be there in difficult times.

Five

We all stood silent in one corner of the college basketball court. Philip had instructed Radha to stay at home. Ballu, Sunil and other members were sitting in the middle. The other students gathered around them. Classrooms were closed; professors were discussing about the forthcoming exams in the staff room. There was a definite uneasiness in the conduct of all students; the hustle and bustle of the college was missing. All were morose and anxious faces; the silence prevailed for quite some time until Sunil decided to break the ice.

'Friends, you all are aware of what happened yesterday, I don't want to repeat it.' All eyes were focused on Sunil while Ballu kept looking down at his feet; his loss was more than anyone in the crowd.

'I request all friends to stand up and observe a two-minute silence to honor the departed souls. Their sacrifice can never be forgotten.' Every one stood up to pay their respects.

'Friends, I know it is a difficult time for all of us', Sunil continued, all were hearing him patiently. 'We all have decided to shut down college, government offices, transport every damn thing till such a time we get justice. From today onwards, it will be a total shutdown and we will move in masses, processions, demonstrations and if required we might have to go for violent protests as well.'

Everybody was silent, a few knew there was cause to stand up but majority wanted a peaceful life, it was irrelevant for them if they were in a separate hill state or not. They knew nothing would change; only a few selected and powerful would gain out of it.

'Sunil, I have a suggestion', I said, looking a bit unsure. 'Is it necessary to go on strike immediately?' I asked, while Sunil and Ballu looked at me trying to figure out what I meant.

'I mean to say, there are hardly any days left for the final exams; the exams will be over in a month or so. I recommend we give the administration two months' notice, by that time those who are appearing in the final year exams can finish their studies and apply for some suitable jobs.'

'Shut up!' Ballu howled. He had not spoken a word until now.

'I know it makes no difference to you, all you are looking at is clearing your exams and running away from this place. I have suffered, and many like me have suffered.'

I kept silent, and looked down in shame.

'It begins tomorrow and let no one have any doubts about it', Ballu made his point clear. There was silence; no one dared to say anything.

'I would like to keep myself out of all this', I said in a faint voice still looking down.

'If you want to run away and hide in your grandpa's lap, go right now. We don't need cowards like you', Ballu was furious and he started towards me. As he was about to grab my collar, Philip came in between.

'Ballu, hold on. Just listen to me for a second', Philip caught Ballu's shoulder and took him to the side. 'Relax, Ballu. I assure you, we are together. I give my word.'

'Philip, go and tell that selfish friend of yours to just get lost from here. We don't need cowards like him.'

'Ballu, try to understand his point. It is not that he is interested only in his motives but there are others who will suffer.

Sunil, just listen to me and analyse the situation', Philip tried to convince Sunil after seeing that Ballu was firm on his decision.

Sunil came towards them, 'Ballu, relax. Let us take a view from others', he said, placing a hand on Ballu's shoulder, consoling him.

'Friends, our suggestion is that we issue a notice that exactly after two months there will be a complete shutdown if our demands are not met. By that time, our exams will be over. We need to take care of others who have already been appointed and just waiting for the exams to get over', Philip said.

There was silence; all expectant eyes were on Philip, Ballu and Sunil. 'Come on, friends, we need to take a call on this. What do you suggest?' Sunil asked.

'I think Philip is right. We can issue a notice and by that time the exams would be over', said a girl standing in one extreme corner.

'Yes, she is right', 'Yes, we need some time…' The call was well supported. Finally, a decision was taken to issue a notice from the students union to the administration and delay the proceedings. Time is a big healer and everyone was hopeful that after two months, the deep scars would heal and people will forget everything. Life has to continue, in pleasure or in pain. The show must go on.

The Uprising had been declared and the entire town was talking about the movement for a separate state. After the incident in Muzaffarnagar, it was clear that people were wounded, not defeated. You trip and fall, but now there were hundreds of hands ready to help the fallen. In the evening, Philip and I were discussing the whole incident with grandpa. After listening to us and our views, which were pro-movement, Grandpa told us something again, giving us examples and extracts from Hindu mythology, the way he always did:

'There are three prominent pillars which support the entire monument of human life and its events. In Hindu religion, we worship them in the form of three supreme Goddesses. The first is Goddess Lakshmi or wealth, the trade factor or the power to buy anything, lure anything. I have seen people enslaved for their entire life to earn a few traces of Lakshmi. So if you have money or wealth, you can buy anything but at the same time you have to be vigilant to protect it. If you don't have this power, then rest assured you will toil day and night to acquire your traces of Lakshmi.' We were listening to every word carefully.

'The second is the Goddess of power or strength. We worship her in the form of Goddess Durga. It signifies energy, the strength that runs the whole world. Without this energy, everything will be still, lifeless. All will be dust. The third is wisdom or Goddesses Saraswati. You may be poor or weak but remember, in the end, he who has wisdom with him wins. Mother Saraswati or wisdom is the most important force in anybody's life. Without wisdom, Lakshmi and Durga become destructive forces. Wealth without wisdom to spend it, and power without the knowledge to understand the responsibility to use it will create havoc. The truth remains unmoved that humans are viewed better than animals but history tells us that they are worse than animals. I don't want to influence young minds with my views but remember, the day the power goes in wrong hands, nothing will be safe.

'Remember one more thing, in all human interactions there is exchange of these three powers. We rarely show that we have these three forces embedded in us but we look forward to acquiring them from external sources. Try and use these forces and see how your life changes. Give the poor the power of Lakshmi with a little prayer that goddess Lakshmi relieves him of his poverty. Assure the weak of the power and the energy of the Almighty and give fools the words of wisdom. Then, you will always be victorious.'

Days passed and things moved on with a normal pace. I got serious with my studies. Philip was free except for a few students who came to the church to learn guitar. The impending situation had taken a toll on the tourist traffic. The shopkeepers and hotels made good money during peak seasons but the movement for a separate hill state and the ongoing agitation had led to a lull as far as tourists were concerned.

Exams were now nearing and the situation seemed like it was getting back to normal. Time is a big healer and it had healed the wounds of those who suffered with the ongoing agitation, although the scars were still visible.

After two weeks of hard studies, the exams were finally over. Philip was satisfied with his performance, thanks to Radha's notes and selective study. Radha and I were confident about scoring good marks.

It's easy to come to this world but to survive amongst millions gets harder and harder. I suddenly realised I must pick up a job to support grandpa, a job where I can earn just about, to gain my grandpa's confidence in me. Philip knew music was his dream, his passion, but getting a break was an uphill task. Radha was worried that soon her father would be looking for a suitable match for her and she would be in an unknown house with unknown people. After exams are over, one thinks that all your worries are over. Only a few realise that difficult times are ahead. Till now, the focus was to study, pass exams and that's all. Now the real struggle was going to begin.

Six

'Vijay, get up! It's already nine, the sun is over head and you are still sleeping!'

I threw the quilt aside and rushed towards the door on hearing Philip's voice. I rubbed my sleepy eyes and opened the door.

'Philip, how come you're here so early?' I asked.

'I've got a surprise for you', Philip wagged a neatly rolled newspaper in front of me.

'What's this?' I inquired.

'Yesterday night Sonia called me', Philip said.

'What's new in that? I'm sure she must be calling you almost every day', my voice dwindled to a whisper.

'This was related to you', Philip remarked. 'She gave me a clue, she told me to have a look at tomorrow's newspaper, especially the magazine section.' My eyes sparkled, I knew what Philip meant.

'Show me!' I said with alacrity. Philip opened the newspaper and showed it to me. My story was published on the front page of the magazine section. I was delighted. I knew it was just the beginning but I had already taken a step towards pursuing my dream. My dream was to become a writer and pursue my career in the world of stories; a mysterious world where all you have to do is dream, be what you want, do what you want.

'Philip, just give me five minutes, I'll get ready', I said, and rushed to the bathroom.

We knocked on the door. Radha was busy dusting the windows in an old tattered *salwar kameez*. Her father was at work. Seeing us, Radha rushed to change. She was very careful about how she presented herself.

'How come you people came without intimation?' Radha asked.

'We are happy you didn't waste time in getting ready', said Philip. 'Now hurry up and get going!' Philip pulled her hand and took her out of the house.

'What are you doing, Philip? I can't go out. I have to cook lunch for my dad and there are other household chores to be done.'

'Don't bother about your drunkard dad. He would prefer a bottle of country liquor than your food', remarked Philip. I resisted the urge to laugh.

'Shut up! Don't speak anything about my dad. You go with your 'tourist friend Sonia', why bother with me?' Radha replied with deceptive grin. Philip pulled her out, picked up the lock kept on the table, locked the door and kept the keys in his pocket.

'What are you doing, Philip? I told you I can't go, I don't want to go', Radha resisted.

'It's for Vijay and not for me. He is taking us out for a treat because today his story got published in the newspaper.' Philip said unfolding the newspaper and showing it to Radha.

'I don't believe it! Show it to me!' Radha said in an excited tone. Her face was glowing with pleasure and elation as she looked at the story in the paper.

'Give me the keys', Radha scowled at Philip.

'No way! You are coming with us', said Philip.

'Stupid, I have to give it to my dad. Who knows how much time we might take to come back?'

Philip smiled and tossed the keys at Radha.

Life was really beautiful. No problems, no ambitions, only dreams in our eyes. My eyes were dreaming about writing stories, true and passionate stories. Philip was dreaming about rocking the world with his music and Radha had a special dream in her eyes: of love, no commitments, and no promises.

'Any news about Sonia?' Radha asked sarcastically. I laughed and winked at Philip.

'She is fine, and mind you, it was me who befriended her. I have an equal share in getting Vijay's story published', Philip remarked.

'Yeah, I do agree', I said.

We packed a few eatables, a few soft drinks and headed towards Lal Tibba. By the time we reached, Philip and Radha were once again engrossed in arguments about Sonia. I grabbed my pen and notebook and started writing something, keeping Radha in mind.

I love you, is what I want to say,
but only if you could listen.
Think of me and read these lines,
In my dreams and prayers you'll be always mine.

When I look into your eyes dark and deep,
A touch of agony and my heart begins to weep.
I look up to the sky and the heavens overhead,
Is it some spell or I'm losing my head.

One day you will feel my presence,
That day you'll desire my skin on you.
One day you will seek my presence
That day I would say... 'I love you'.

'Where are you lost, Vijay? What you are writing, show it to me', said Radha.

'Nothing', I closed the notebook. I did not want anyone to know about my feelings, especially Radha. The sun was behind the hills, a few stars started to twinkle in the sky. We headed towards home with a thousand dreams in our eyes.

Every day, my routine was set. The day began with morning *shlokas* and hymns from my grandpa's morning rituals. Every morning by 5am, Grandpa was up and awake. Irrespective of the weather being good or bad, there would be no change in grandpa's routine. He would wake up even if he was down with fever or there was a snow blizzard outside. His day started with a small prayer in our house, and then he would prepare tea for himself and me. After that, he went to the temple. This routine was fixed and my body was well-versed with it.

Our bodies and mind adapt to certain things, which they sense as routine. That morning too, everything was the same, except for Grandpa's *shlokas* and hymns breaking the silence of the room; Grandpa was not in the room. Something was wrong; my mind assured me everything was fine, but the goosebumps on my skin disagreed.

I looked for Grandpa in the room. Finding him nowhere, I went to the bathroom. The bathroom door was latched from inside, I figured Grandpa was in there but it was unusual for him to be in the bathroom for so long.

'Are you all right, Grandpa?'

Knock...knock...knock!

'What happened, Grandpa? Is everything OK?'

'Vijay, something is wrong with me. I am unable to get up. For past one hour I have been trying to get up but my body is not responding.'

'Can you open the latch, Grandpa?'

'Let me try if somehow I can drag myself and unlatch the door.' After some effort, Grandpa was able to open the door. I burst into tears when I saw Grandpa wrapped in a thin cotton sheet lying on the floor and looking helplessly towards me. I could sense he was feeling sorry for me. I tried to lift him off the floor but he was too heavy for me. I rushed outside and called Santu to help me. We put Grandpa on the bed and Santu rushed to call the doctor.

Doctor Kakar confirmed that it was a paralytic attack and Grandpa was required to be admitted to a hospital immediately. As soon as Philip came to know about the incident, he rushed to my place. He arranged for a taxi and grandpa was admitted in the hospital. The paralytic attack had affected his neurons, which had led to some portion in the brain malfunctioning. The left side of his body was paralyzed. The doctors were unable to do much about it. Our relatives from Dehradun came down to help but all we could do was pray to God; wait and hope that things will be all right.

After four days, the doctors confirmed that his vital organs had stopped working and it was just a matter of time now as to how many days Grandpa would survive. Grandpa refused to die in a hospital bed, he desired to be taken home. The next day his condition worsened; he was unable to speak now. I remember that same night, Philip and I were sitting next to Grandpa, we were afraid to leave him because some sense of security prevailed that death would not dare to touch Grandpa till such a time we were guarding him. The whole night we were awake, by his side, trying to guard him from the angels of death. Grandpa kept looking at me and at times looked at Philip as if he was telling Philip to take care of me after he was gone.

In the early hours of morning, I don't know how it happened but I still remember the dream, I still wonder how I went off to sleep.

I opened my eyes; someone held my shoulder and ran his fingers on my forehead. I raised my head and looked up, still sitting next to Grandpa. It was daylight and the sun was rising in the Far East, across the horizon. I saw my grandfather standing in front of me, covering the sun which was directly in my face.

'Don't worry, my child. Everything will be all right. Do your duty for which God has sent you.'

'Grandpa, are you all right? You were not well, and see, Philip is also here to look after you.' I asked, raising my head to have a clear look at Grandpa, my eyes still half-open.

'Grandpa, I want to see you, please. This sun is directly in my eyes.' I got up; the sun still in my eyes. I tried to see properly but the rays of the sun were too bright for me to see anything.

'Grandpa... grandpa... grandpa!'

I woke up hearing Philip shout.

I knew it was all over, Grandpa had left us.

I experienced the worst feeling ever in life: the moment I carried my Grandpa's body on my shoulders. I realised I was a grown man now. All my life, my grandpa had carried me on his shoulders but today, my shoulders had found a new kind of burden on it. More than the sorrow of losing Grandpa was the realisation that I was left alone in this world to fend for myself. People were there to support me but I knew it was only a short-term association to console me. Kumar *sahib* agreed to let me live in the same outhouse till such a time that I was self-sufficient. My Grandpa's brother also helped me but he had his own family and priorities to look after; life cannot wait and come to a halt. The show must go on.

We often don't appreciate what we have until it's gone. Till the moment Grandpa left me, I thought he would always be there. Now I understood that nothing in life should be taken for granted, including those who love you. Life can change instantly. Life taught me two great lessons that day: first, I realised life doesn't stop even though I never imagined a life without Grandpa, but life has to go on and on. It doesn't make a difference and no one cares whether we exist or not. The world will continue to turn without our awkward presence.

The second great lesson life taught me was that it introduced me to friendship. I cannot explain what friendship is. I would only say friendship is Philip and Philip is friendship. Philip never left me; he was standing by my side at every moment. He was the only shoulder available for me to cry on.

'I don't know, Philip', I said, taking a deep breath. 'I really don't know how I will manage all by myself without Grandpa; I can imagine nothing without him.'

'Don't worry, let's go out and get some fresh air.'

Radha was waiting for us at Picture Palace. I saw her and looked deep into her eyes but was unable to say anything. I wanted to say something but I began to choke on my words so I preferred to keep quiet.

'Don't worry, Vijay, everything will be all right', Radha said, hugging me. This was the first time any kind of affection was portrayed by Radha towards me. I wanted to hug her hard and cry out loud, but I didn't move. I knew Radha's love would melt me and it would be difficult for me to control my tears. I gently pushed her away.

'I'm okay, Radha, don't worry.'

We sat at that bench for hours. Philip tried to entertain me so that I would feel better. He bought coffee, then popcorn and then fruit juice, but it was difficult for me to swallow anything.

In the evening, we went back. Philip decided to stay with me till I was feeling better. Every night, Radha would send us dinner – home-cooked food. This was the first time we realised Radha was a good cook. Although life was slowly getting back on track because of Philip and Radha, I missed Grandpa whenever I was alone. Now I knew what it meant to be an orphan.

Next day, while we were returning from the mall road after a stroll, we saw Ballu, Sunil and other members of the students union gathered at a tea stall.

'Hey Philip, can I have a word with you, brother? Get Vijay also along with you', Sunil shouted, seeing us walking down the narrow alley. Philip knew it was an unwarranted call, but he would have to attend to them.

'Radha, you move on, we might have to spend some time with them', Philip said. Radha left for home while we walked towards Sunil.

'Hi Philip, hello Vijay', Sunil greeted us and we shook hands with everyone in turn.

'Vijay, I heard about Grandpa, really sad news', said Sunil. 'If you require anything, do let me know and believe me, I am just one phone call away, available 24X7.'

'Definitely, Sunil. Thank you for your concern', I replied.

'Philip, I called you because tomorrow the two months deadline given by the students union gets over', Sunil said, while Philip gave him a tolerant hearing.

'Philip, from tomorrow onwards we are declaring a complete shutdown. The demonstration and processions begin at ten in the morning. I hope that both of you will join us.'

'Sunil, as you already know, Vijay's grandpa left us recently. We are disturbed and I would request you that we may be excused.'

'Yes, we understand and Vijay can be excused, but Philip, we need you', said Ballu.

'Ballu, try to understand our condition, I cannot leave Vijay. As it is, we are going through a rough patch and moreover I can't be roaming the streets when Vijay needs me.'

'I lost my brother, Philip. He died fighting for our rights, our *Devbhoomi*. How you can say such a thing?' Ballu looked at us with crinkled eyes and a frowning face.

'Vijay's grandfather was an old man who died a natural death.'

'Ballu, mind your words. How dare you speak anything about Grandpa? Don't!' Philip looked at Ballu with fiery eyes.

'Don't you stare at me, Philip. It was because of you and Vijay that we decided to delay our movement; else we would have achieved our goal by now.'

'It is your battle; fight it at your might.'

'Philip, it's for our *Devbhoomi*.'

'Why do you want to trouble others? We are not interested in your separate state ideology.'

'It's not an 'ideology', but rights for everyone.'

'Whatever it may be, we are not getting involved.'

'So if it is an ego issue, then let me cut it short. I want to see both of you tomorrow, else I will chew your bones.' Ballu was furious; he was staring hard into Philip's eyes. He gave a stern look at me. I was panicky; there was definitely fear in my eyes. I knew Ballu's temper had a bad reputation.

'Come on, touch me and I'll show you what your worth is', Philip said.

'Philip!' Ballu shrieked and charged towards him. I came in between and held Ballu.

'Ballu, brother, please listen to me. I promise we will be there. Calm down', I said, consoling him.

'I promise you, Ballu, we will be there.'

'Tell your friend to behave with me, else someday I will break his neck!' shouted Ballu, staring hard at Philip.

Philip said nothing. He turned around and walked away from the tea stall before there was anymore ruckus. I rushed towards Philip, who was fuming. As far as I knew, Philip was a guy with lots of patience. He would rarely lose his cool about any issue. This was probably the first time I had seen him furious.

For five minutes, neither of us spoke a word. Philip was fuming and I knew it was better to keep quiet until Philip calmed down. After walking in silence for some time, Philip spoke:

'Why did you butt in?'

'The fight was not required.'

'I would have showed him his worth.'

'Just let it go, Philip.'

'Ballu thinks just because he is the college president, he is a demi God?'

'Philip, what's the use of fighting like brats in the middle of the market?'

'Then you think it is okay to walk the streets with banners in our hands? I'm not convinced with his movement for a separate state. These are all political stunts to gain mileage out of.'

'No, we will not move with banners. We will be present and move with them. We won't be in the limelight; we will place ourselves in one corner and that's all.'

'Do whatever you want, I'm not coming', Philip remarked with disgusted look. I knew Philip would not leave me alone, he was going to be there.

Seven

I locked the door. Philip had forgotten whatever had happened the previous evening and was whistling in a carefree manner. We sprinted across the alley and reached Gandhi Chowk, where all the demonstrators were beginning to gather.

The word had spread across town that the struggle for a separate hill state will kick off again and this time with added momentum. It was time to do or die. It was agreed that we would all meet at Gandhi Chowk and march with banners and hoardings up to the park, where a huge rally will be held. The other group of demonstrators were joining from the other part of the town, Landour.

People started pouring in. No one expected five thousand people would gather from Gandhi Chowk alone. It was indeed a complete shutdown. All shops, government offices, roadways, buses, everything was down. Sharp at nine, the demonstrators started marching towards the park. Everyone was shouting slogans, demanding their right for a separate hill state. There was news that their leader, Shekhar Singh, had already started on a tour of every village and town of the hill area. He was the director of this movement, with others following his ideology.

'Did you hear the news, Philip?' I said, moving with the crowd in the last lot.

'What news?' inquired Philip.

'Shekhar Singh will be addressing the rally tomorrow at the park.'

'Vijay, I'm somehow not really convinced with all these movements and demonstrations. The poor people look for their bread and butter. All other issues are irrelevant for them.'

'I believe a separate hill state will guarantee many educated youths a job somewhere. We are nationalists; the only thing we demand is recognition and our rights. No development has taken place in this area post-independence', I said.

'I really don't know, Vijay. Only time will tell.'

The demonstrators reached the park. Two more groups joined in from Landour. The strength of demonstrators was almost ten thousand plus. For a small hill town like Mussoorie, it was a positive indication as far as this movement was concerned.

At one end of the park, on a raised sort of platform, Prem Prakash was already standing with a mike in his hand. Prem Prakash was Sunil's dad. He was sixty-years-old, a little stout but with a magnetic personality. Mr Prem Prakash had a wise and benevolent appearance in spite of the fact that he never shaved. He had the charm to enrapture any crowd with ease.

The crowd began to settle down. We adjusted ourselves a little away from the crowd, at the railing. The stage was clearly visible from there and we were comfortable being a little away from the crowd. Ballu, Sunil and other members of the students union settled down on the floor immediately in front of the platform.

Ballu was often referred to as 'The bull'. The reason was that he lacked intelligence, but he was universally respected for the steadiness of his character, tremendous strength and short temper. Sunil was sharp, he would evaluate the pros and cons of the situation before taking any step, and he also knew the importance of using the right words.

All those who had taken part in the procession were now all in the park. When Prem Prakash saw that they were waiting attentively, he checked the mike and cleared his throat. He began his speech with a slogan.

'I bow my head to pray for my *Devbhoomi* and my head stands tall to mention those who have laid their lives for our *Devbhoomi*.' All eyes and ears were focused towards Prem Prakash.

'My brothers and sisters of *Devbhoomi*, last night I had a strange dream. I saw the daughters of mother Ganga, Mandakini and Alaknanda, bonded in chains. Their water, crimson red and blood flowing from their eyes. I asked, "Mother Ganga, what has happened to you?" She replied that she has lost her virginity, the symbol of purity. She asked me, "son, will you help me so that I may regain my identity and purity?" She told me to look at the blood streaming down the flowing water, which would taint the entire *Devbhoomi*.' Prem Prakash took a long pause.

'The dream was disturbing and I woke up profusely sweating and shivering. I went to my temple and lit a lamp there. I promised the Almighty that my struggle will continue even if I have to die a thousand deaths. The struggle is not for me but for all the people of *Devbhoomi*. I ask you, my fellow men, are you all with me or do I have to fight this battle alone?'

'We are all with you! We are all with you!' the crowd roared. The cry was deafening.

'I just wanted to hear that from you all. Day after tomorrow, our leader Shekhar Singh will be in Mussoorie and will address you all. I would request all men, women, and children to gather here. It's time that our cries are heard in Delhi or they should be prepared to face the consequences.'

Someone shouted from the center, '*Jai ho, Devbhoomi!*' and the crowd roared in unison.

'*Jai ho, Devbhoomi! Jai ho, Devbhoomi!*'

One of the protesters in the front row cleared his throat and began to sing a highland folk song. It was a hymn for the gods and goddesses of *Devbhoomi*. His voice was hoarse, but he sang well, well enough to stir the crowd with him.

'*I pray to my god's*

I pray to my goddesses.

Sanctify all my people,

Sanctify the Devbhoomi.'

The crowd marched out singing the song in unison. The singing of the song threw everyone in a wild excitement. Even the most tuneless of them had picked up the tune and they were singing out loud. Prem Prakash's speech had given them a completely new outlook. They did not know how far their rebellious attitude could sustain and how far they could go to achieve their aim. They had no reason to think about whether their protests were called for a purpose, or a separate state will in fact solve their problems. But one thing was clear: they were prepared for it.

The work of organising the next day's show fell on the students union. A few intellectuals amongst the group elaborated the complete revolution under one name '*Jagran*' or the awakening. Initially, a few were against this movement. They were of the thought that their identity was India and the biggest thing that mattered was being Indian. Their loyalty towards the nation was foremost and the struggle for a separate state was considered a separatist viewpoint. But now, the winds were changing. Fight for your right, else perish. Make your identity, or get buried under the might of those who have the power to rule.

Philip was still not convinced but decided to go with the majority and be a part of the demonstrations, just to make the others feel that he was with them. I had already changed my mind, my heart and soul was for the movement. That evening again, Radha had come with dinner for us. While I came in from the kitchen, I heard some faint arguing between Radha and Philip about something. I saw Philip holding her hand and then he gently kissed her lips. I don't know why, but that sight changed my expression and I turned around and went back inside the kitchen. I could hear my heart pounding with anger and I could feel the blood rushing through my veins. *What is the matter with me? Why am I behaving in a strange manner?* I explained to myself that they probably love each other so why should I feel bad? But I knew I could not let Radha go from my life even for Philip's sake. I also know I must do something to win my love over, but how? I had no idea. No it would not be correct, I was being selfish. Philip was my friend and he has been the one who has stood by me in difficult times. I can sacrifice anything for him, even my love. After that moment, I decided not to think anymore about Radha, she would just be a fairytale fantasy for me and will remain only in my dreams, and that was the reality.

Eight

After a long, tiring and tensed day preparing for the huge rally with the students union, we reached home. I poured a cup of tea for Philip and myself in steel tumblers. Philip pulled out two plastic chairs and placed them out in the veranda overlooking the Kumar Villa. The dim light from the street lamp reflected on the front portion of Kumar Villa. It was twilight and the stars were popping out slowly in the sky, as we settled and sipped the hot, sweet tea. Philip had to go to Radha's house to get our packed dinner but he was too tired to go all the way to Gandhi Chowk. We decided instead, to just have a glass of milk and bread for the night.

I was looking into the sky the moon was half-crescent while the stars were twinkling in the clear sky. I thought about Grandpa, I knew his soul would be somewhere near by me. There was silence; both of us were engrossed in our own world. We were listening to the constant chirping of cricket and the occasional rustling of the leaves.

After finishing our tea, we went inside. Philip was tired and fell flat on the bed. He closed his eyes for a while, and then he was staring at the ceiling. I pulled out my old diary, which I used to write poems and stories in. I had not written a word for a long time. Initially, I was busy with exams and later, Grandpa's death had taken a toll on my creativity. I opened the notebook to a clean page and pulled out a pencil and an eraser from the drawer. I always use a pencil to write with, it gives me the freedom to erase and correct my mistakes.

I wish life was that simple too. I sharpened a pencil and scribbled a few lines.

I opened the window for some fresh air and some fresh ideas to flow in. I looked at Philip; he looked like he was engrossed in his own world of thoughts.

'Philip, what's going in your mind?' I asked. My words startled Philip.

'Nothing important', he replied.

'Come on, tell me. It might give me some idea for my next story.'

'Then you should guess what's on my mind.'

'If I'm right, you are thinking about Sonia.'

'No, I'm thinking about Radha.' As soon as he completed his sentence, there was a soft knock on the door. It was as if someone was trying to sneak in without making much noise.

I got up and went towards the door to see who it could be. Philip also got up and looked towards the door.

'Who's there?' I asked suspiciously.

'Don't shout! It's me, Radha.'

I quickly opened the door.

'Are you crazy? How come you are here at this hour of night?' Philip said, puzzled.

'I was waiting for you. Why didn't you come to take your dinner?' She held out the tiffin and handed it to me.

'You are really a foolish girl. What if your dad comes to know?' I said.

'Don't worry, he is already fast asleep.'

'Down with a bottle of country liquor in his belly', added Philip.

'Shut up!' Radha remarked, hastily.

Radha went to the kitchen and warmed the food. She came back with two plates in her hand that had the food neatly laid out: lentils, fried potatoes and *chapattis*. I unrolled a jute mat, placed it on the floor and we sat crossed legged. We were in fact famished after the long day and pounced on the plate like hungry dogs. Radha watched us carefully, like a mother watches her children eat food. It gave Radha a lot of satisfaction to watch us relish food cooked by her. To me, she was a friend I can depend upon.

After dinner, Radha picked up the used plates and rinsed them. She cleaned the gas stove and washed the mopping cloth. By the time she was done, it was already 10pm.

'I think, Radha, you should stay here for the night. As it is, things are not on track in town. Someone might see you and cook up some sour tale', Philip said.

'I will wake you early in the morning around four and you can be home by the time your father wakes up', I reassured her.

And so it was decided that Radha should stay for the night. I placed a mattress for Philip and myself in one corner while Radha was given the bed to sleep on. Philip was already quite sleepy and within minutes he was fast asleep, snoring away to glory.

I opened my diary once again and continued with my story. After a while, I watched Philip carefully, he was sleeping like a child. His mouth was a little open and he was breathing quite fast. I looked at Radha, she was still awake, admiring the wall with patches of uneven plaster at many places.

'Radha, you are still awake?'

'It's difficult for me to sleep in a new place', she said.

'Shall we sit outside?'

'I think so.'

I took a blanket and we went outside. We sat on the plastic chairs, placing our feet on the railing. We could see the stars, the crescent moon and the valley with a few scattered lights from the small veranda. Radha pointed to the moon.

'I feel life is incomplete in all aspects like this half-moon', she said.

'You sound quite philosophical; I thought you were a stupid girl.'

'These stars are responsible for creating unrest in one's life and my dad says if they were not there then there would have been no trouble in the world', Radha said, looking up towards the mysterious sky, vast and never-ending.

'Your alcoholic dad also speaks in a philosophical way.'

'Vijay, whatever he might be, I love him. I know he doesn't care about me but I care for my dad. He was not the same, everything changed when my mother left us, and he became a different man altogether. First, it was painful to lose someone whom you love so much and more than that, shame and disgrace that you have to face from rest of the world.'

'You think these stars are responsible for all misfortunes and sorrows in our life?' I asked her.

'No, I have a second theory. When someone close to you dies, a star is formed. That's why there are countless stars in the sky.' I remembered that's what grandpa used to tell me when I was a child.

'Who told you this tale?'

'I remember when I was a little girl, my mother used to show me the brightest star and tell me that the brightest star was my granny, my mother's mom.' She took a long pause. All parents somehow tell a similar tale to bluff their children. Now that was amazing, I thought.

'I believe ten years from now, you will also be telling the same story to your daughter.'

'No, I might not tell the same thing to my daughter. I might tell her that the major share belongs to the darkness and not the stars.' I went close to her and carefully placed the blanket around her and placed my arm around her shoulder.

'So you think when we die, we either become a star or will be lost in darkness?' I asked her, looking up towards the sky.

'I don't know, but I feel that I will become a star the day I die. I will watch you and Philip from there', Radha said, pointing towards the sky.

'Both of you will gaze at my shine in your lonely nights. You will miss me, won't you?' she said, gently placing her head on my shoulder.

'Yes, we will but I would pray that we live together, always. You, me and Philip. We three share a small world and there is no place for anyone else in our world. When our time comes, we will perish together', I said, and gently ran my fingers through her hair.

The moon peeped from the sky, teasing me by reflecting on Radha's beautiful face. The countless stars were still shining in the sky and Radha was comfortably asleep on my shoulder. I never moved an inch, afraid that my slightest of movement might disturb her. I kept looking at Radha; there was an unknown joy to watch her sleep on my shoulder. A conflict was going on in my mind; at one end there was Philip who loved Radha, and on the other end was my love, my passion and all my dreams. *How could I let her go?* I asked myself. The conflict continued and the moon changed its course.

I was keeping track of time. Sharp at four, I moved my hand. The movement was enough to wake her up.

'It's time for you to go', I said.

'It's four o' clock?' inquired Radha.

'Yes.'

'I don't know how come I was fast asleep out in the open. Were you also asleep?'

'Yes, I woke up just now, with you.'

I accompanied Radha till Gandhi Chowk, dropped her at the beginning of the alley and straightaway went to the temple where Grandpa had served God for many years as a priest. It was time for me to ask for something from God, if not the fruit of my ablutions then a reward for Grandpa's service to the almighty. Radha was the only thing on my mind and I knew that until Philip was there, I would never be able to win her love. Last night had made me weak and

I realised that I need her, no matter what it took. I bowed in front of God and made a wish. Then, I got a bit scared. I remembered what Grandpa had told me: *'Whenever you ask something from God, be careful. You never know which one of your wishes may come true. Remember, what you sow, so shall you reap.'*

Nine

By morning, the news of Shekhar Singh addressing a grand rally at the park had spread all over town like wildfire. The members of the students union had pasted posters all over the town. Ten o' clock was the time decided to assemble at the park. The other party workers were responsible for making seating arrangement for prominent leaders. People were moving in masses; never had such a large crowd gathered at Gandhi Chowk before. It seemed like all doors were locked and everyone, the young, the old, women, children, indeed everyone were seen in the streets. I had faith that mere numbers will give strength to the movement. On the contrary, it was seen that men in crowds are more foolish, more violent and more cruel than men separate and alone.

People had assembled with the wildest excitement. They were there for their leader, Shekhar Singh. Sunil and his father, Prem Prakash, were missing. As the crowd reached the park, they saw policemen standing all over the place. A few had wooden sticks in their hands while a majority of them had rifles slung across their shoulders. The police did not challenge the mob but stood at their dedicated places.

The crowd gathered from different directions and the strength of demonstrators was soon unmanageable. We stood by the same place where we were during the previous rally. It was slightly away but had a good view of the stage. Everyone waited for their leader to arrive but after waiting patiently for an hour, the crowd was growing restless. Then, rumours of Shekhar Singh being arrested started spreading among the corwd.

Soon, a confirmation came Prem Prakash had also been arrested by the police at his residence for giving a provocative speech the previous week. The second piece of news was even worse for the protesters. In fact, Shekhar Singh was arrested twenty kilometers short of Mussoorie, at Rajpur; he was not allowed to come to Mussoorie as a precautionary measure.

After some time, the Deputy Superintendent of police, Vikram Singh, addressed the crowd from the stage:

'I request all people to disperse from this place. Section 44 has been imposed and any kind of gathering is unlawful. I give everyone precisely ten minutes to disperse off peacefully, else the police will have to use force.'

Ballu's facial expressions were changing. 'I will not go anywhere and no one will go. If these men in uniform have the guts, then try and move us.'

Ballu started moving towards the stage.

'I warn you, do not try to provoke the crowd. Else, we might have to stop you by using force.'

'What are you waiting for? Come on, stop me if you can!' Ballu was crazy.

'I know no one can stop us now. It is the awakening, and this is the strength of unity of the *Devbhoomi*.'

The crowd roared and clapped after Ballu's remark. We were getting restless; we never expected that things might start to go out of hand. Philip looked anxiously towards the stage where Ballu was moving. I was nervous.

'Philip, let's move out of here. I can sense trouble', I said, looking sheepishly towards Philip.

'Vijay, I must stop Ballu. He is a crazy guy and you know how short-tempered he is.'

'Hold on, Philip. We should stay out of this ruckus.'

Ballu went up to the center stage and held the mike.

'I warn you get off the stage', cautioned the Deputy Superintendent of Police. Four armed men went ahead. They removed their rifles from their shoulder.

'See! They want to kill me!' howled Ballu.

'This is my final warning. Get off the stage. Right now.'

'Come on, shoot me if you can. Come on, shoot me!' shouted Ballu.

'Vijay, I should get Ballu off the stage. He is trying to provoke the police.'

'Leave it, Philip. It's not safe', I held his hand.

'My dear fellowmen, if it's a battle, them I'm here standing and declaring a war for our rights. I will not move from this stage and if anyone has the guts then come here and throw me out!' Ballu shouted, looking towards the Superintendent of Police, challenging him.

The armed constables aimed the rifles towards Ballu; all eyes were on the scene unfolding on the stage. Their hearts were beating like an express train. Was this even real?

'Today the authorities have challenged us, they want to see how serious we are with our demands. They have arrested our leaders, Shekhar Singh and Prem Prakash. Now they are threatening us!'

The armed constables cocked their 303 rifle, their barrel pointing directly towards Ballu, aiming at his chest.

'Come on, if you want to shoot, shoot! Make another grave for innocent people like you did in Muzaffarnagar!' Ballu screamed, showing his chest to the armed constables.

'Get off or the constables will shoot you!' roared the Superintendent of police.

'If you want to move me, then kill me!' shouted Ballu, throwing the mike at the armed constables with all his might.

'Shoot me, you cowards... come on, shoot me!' Ballu once again showed his chest to the constables standing in front of him aiming at him with cocked weapon.

Thak!

A loud burst engulfed Ballu's voice; everyone was stunned. No one expected that the police would really open fire. Till now, it seemed like a drama but it was real. No one moved. All eyes were focused on Ballu. He fell on his knees, blood oozing out from his chest.

'Ballu…!' Philip cried out loud.

He jumped off the railing freeing his grip from my hand. He ran towards Ballu to help him.

'Someone call the ambulance fast... Get out of my way!' Philip ran fearlessly towards Ballu pushing a group of men standing in his way.

Philip ran towards the stage and climbed up to comfort Ballu. 'Someone call the ambulance hurry up!' Philip screamed.

The other armed constable aimed, this time the barrel was pointing at Philip. Unmindful of any other thing but to save Ballu, Philip tried to lift Ballu who was now soaked in his own blood but still breathing.

Thak!

Another bullet was fired. This time it was Philip; the bullet hit him in his stomach. Philip fell down gripping his stomach. A stream of crimson red blood oozed out from his belly.

'Philip!' I shouted but I was too afraid to go towards him. The crowd was horrified. Men, women, and children, everyone started screaming and running in different directions. They knew that anyone could be shot. It was chaos everywhere, frightened faces screaming and running for their lives. My first instinct was to rush and save Philip, but I was too frightened to do anything. I jumped and slid under a concrete bench shivering; all I could hear were cries and shrieks of people running in panic. I heard a few more shots fired. I looked towards the stage; I could see Ballu lying flat on his belly while Philip was moving slowly trying to find someone. Was Philip trying to look out for me? After struggling for some time, he gave up. His body all soaked in blood while his eyes were still searching for someone.

I got out from my hiding place and tried to reach out for Philip. Then something hit my head from behind. I fell on my knees, darkness surrounding my eyes.

Ten

This was the first time I was attending a funeral and so was Radha. Philip was asleep, forever, inside the coffin; the coffin, covered with flowers and wreaths. It was a small funeral – only a few Patrician's' Brothers and Sisters along with Father Thomas were at the graveyard, dressed in black robes. Brother Thomas, with the help of few locals had organised Philip's cremation ceremony at the local graveyard of YWCA. He had taken special permission from the authorities. After yesterday's incident, a curfew had been imposed in the city.

The coffin was placed inside the earth and covered with mud. *Ashes to ashes, dust to dust, may the departed soul rest in peace.* We watched the proceedings; we were all in a shock, hoping it was all a bad dream and when we'd wake up, everything would be the way it was. Neither Radha nor I shed a tear. We stood there like stone, still not able to deal with what had actually come about.

However, the horrors hadn't stopped there. After the firing incident, the mob had become more violent. The police station at Landour was reduced to ashes. The deputy superintendent of police, Vikram Singh was caught by the mob and mauled to death. The queen of hills had lost its charm; it was now dripping in crimson blood.

After the cremation, I never spoke a word and just went home. Once or twice, Radha tried to console me and condemn the incident but I was still in a state of shock, expressionless like a stone. I closed all the doors and drew all the curtains so that not even a ray of light could enter; I switched off all the lights and sat on the bed with my knees drawn to my chest. A sudden outburst overpowered me and I wept out the sorrow of losing my friend. For a long time, I sat with my head between my knees and cried like a child. The question I was asking myself again and again was *Did Philip die because of me?*

Two days passed and I never moved from my room. My mind constantly visualising how Philip was killed, Philip's eyes searching for me. People's cries, the chaos and the sound of bullets being fired humming in my ears. I felt losing Philip was my fault; I wish I could have convinced him to stay back. Philip never even wanted to be a part of the revolution; I should have held his hand tight enough that he would have stayed there for another minute. I should have never allowed him to rush like that. I can't believe he rushed to help Ballu – the same Ballu who was threatening him a few days back.

These thoughts were taking a toll on me; I stopped speaking to anyone and hardly went out. A week passed and the curfew was still in place. It was lifted for two-hours every day for people to get important commodities. I was latched inside, weak, feeble, depressed, and lonely. After Philip's death, everything had changed; the world seemed to be different altogether. Philip, Radha and I, we had a small world of our own, which had been shattered and there was no way to complete it. Philip was our strength, the axis on which our world had revolved until now.

More than losing my friend, I was feeling sorry for Radha. She was Philip's everything. Her love was as sacred as Philip's courage and as tainted as his identity. They were not in a relationship in the eyes of the public but they were definitely in love. After Philip, she was shattered. But life has to continue. The pain of losing a loved one will always be felt. The wounds will heal with time but the scars will remain forever.

Soon, the debris of the burning city cooled and so did the flames of rage inside the hearts of the protesters. The Government included the agenda for a separate hill state and an assurance was given to include the bill in next parliament session. The queen of hills was once again breathing fresh air; the smoke of agitation and hatred was evaporating. Shops opened, schools colleges opened and people were once again seen on the mall road. Some still had sorrow on their faces while others were grateful about the dark clouds having passed by. Radha applied for a job at one of the primary schools and kept herself busy with little children. She always searched for Philip in them, in their giggles, in their poems, in their play fields. I realised I should take up some job to keep myself alive as well.

My financial constraints forced me to pick a part time job at one of the hotels. I was also taking tuitions for school children in the morning from six to eight and in the evening I would be at the front desk of a hotel, handling all sorts of customers. There were businessmen, honeymoon couples, college brats, and others who were there, hiding from the world behind the closed doors.

My home was about two miles from the hotel, but if I took a shorter route that went via the Camel's Back Road, I saved on about half a mile of walking. Camel's Back Road was a lonely road and the only visible thing on that one-mile long forlorn track was a huge bungalow that belonged to

Mrs. Castellino. It was called the Summer Hall Cottage and Mrs. Castellino lived in it all by herself. She never had any friends or relatives in India. After her husband's death, Major Castellino, an officer in the British Indian Army, Mrs. Castellino decided to stay back, alone, in the bungalow. All she survived on was the pension of her dead husband and a cat that kept her company.

That day, after sickening and tiresome seven hours at the front desk, I was trudging along the desolate Camel's Back Road. I was walking in carefree manner, thinking about hot food and my warm, cozy bed to sleep on as soon as I reached home. Then, something unusual caught my attention. I heard a strange sound, like somebody crying at a distance. I tried to concentrate on the sound and tried to follow it. My steps were leading towards Summer Hall Cottage, the huge bungalow where Mrs. Castellino lived. For some reason it felt like a familiar sound, a sobbing cry of a lady in deep pain, something that I seemed to have heard before.

After putting a little more strain on my memory, I remembered. Before I could be sure of the sound I had goosebumps all over. These sounds were the sobbing cries of Mrs. Castellino. I had heard it a couple of days ago – day before yesterday, when I was walking to the hotel, I had heard similar sobbing cries from Mrs. Castellino's house. I had gone inside to ask her if she needed some help. The door was open; Mrs. Castellino was lying on her bed. She was an old lady; probably ninety-years-old.

'Mrs. Castellino, are you all right?' I asked the old lady.

'My son, for past two days I have been down with fever. My body is aching badly and I can't even get up from my bed.' She took a long pause while I stood besides her, thinking about how difficult it is to survive on your own when you are old. Her condition reminded me of my grandfather: old, weak, poor and helpless.

'Son, would you do me a favor?' she asked.

'Yes, Mrs. Castellino. Tell me.'

'Would you call the doctor?'

'Sure, I'll go and call him right now.' I left from there but then decided to call the doctor in the morning; I was already late to report at the hotel and could not waste my time or I would have to stay back for a few more hours.

The next morning it slipped my mind that I had to call the doctor.

I was reminded of my blunder when I had heard the cries again. I was horrified and then after some introspection, I concluded it was all in my mind. Maybe I was a bit tired after a busy routine. I continued home. After dinner I went to bed, but today I was unable to sleep peacefully. The sobbing cries kept drumming in my ears and Mrs. Castellino's image was lingering on my mind; her reflection pleading me to call the doctor or she would die. That whole night, the old lady must have been looking towards the door, waiting for the doctor. A sense of guilt started to prevail in me. The incident also reminded me of Philip, how much of a coward I had been. Philip's eyes had been searching for me in his last moments but I never had the guts to go and help him.

The next day was a busy day again; seven hours at the front desk, without a break. I was handling customers and attending their calls. During peak season, the workload increases and all hotels are flooded with tourists. After my hectic schedule, I was once again on Camel's Back Road, going home. I'd not thought about Mrs. Castellino until I approached her house. Once again, I heard those sobbing cries; all my senses were alert and a current ran down my spine.

I hurried towards home and took a deep breath only after I'd crossed Camel's Back Road. After that day, I never took that road home, even if I had to walk that extra half-mile. A week passed by and I forgot about Mrs. Castellino and her sobbing cries. Then on the seventh day, the skies broke loose and it rained heavily throughout the night. The result of the heavy downpour was that the route which I now took home, was blocked. Now, the route was under repair and would reopen only after a month if the municipality got down to seriously repairing the track.

I didn't have an option but to take Camel's Back Road to go home. The mere thought of Mrs. Castellino and her sobbing cries made me restless. The other thing that I visualised every time I heard those sobbing cries was Philip, but I didn't have another option. As I approached Summer Hall Cottage, I heard those sobbing cries again. I was afraid to even look towards the cottage. I ran towards home shivering and sweating in fear. That whole night, again, I was unable to sleep. The only thing that was on my mind was the weak and feeble face of Mrs. Castellino and those sobbing cries ringing in my ears interspersed with the nightmarish scenes when Philip was shot by the police.

As days passed, the situation got worse. Those cries were now more prevalent on my mind. I could hear them during tuitions and I heard them at work. All I could think about was Mrs. Castellino and Philip. A sense of constant guilt prevailed within me. I knew Mrs. Castellino was ill and in pain. I should have shown urgency and called the doctor at that very moment. Immediate medical comfort might have saved Mrs. Castellino for a few more years. I could have tried to save my friend, not let him rush towards Ballu. Now I feared that I was losing my mind, some unknown power was punishing me.

My behavioral pattern started changing. I rarely get annoyed about any issue, but now lost my cool with petty issues. I was unable to sleep or eat properly. Most of the time I was alone, constantly thinking about Mrs. Castellino and Philip and those sobbing cries echoing in my ears.

I decided to discuss the matter with Radha. I was sure she would understand. I was afraid to mention anything to anyone else; people might have thought I was mad. I waited for Radha at her school gate. I saw the little children run down the play field on the final bell. They rushed to their parents who were at the gate to receive them. This reminded me of my childhood, my grandpa used to come every day to receive me at school.

After all the children had left, Radha came out with a couple more teachers accompanying her. She was dressed in a plain, sky-blue suit, and no makeup, her hair tied carelessly. Radha had always been particular about her looks but after Philip, she had no purpose to put on makeup or look attractive.

'Radha!' I called her, until now she had not noticed me. It took her by surprise.

'Vijay, you are here? I didn't know you were waiting.'

'Nothing, Radha. I just thought of having lunch with you.'

'Is everything all right?'

'Nothing to worry, Radha. It's been quite some time since we'd met, so I thought about seeing you.'

'Anytime, Vijay.'

We went to our favorite Chinese restaurant and ordered lunch.

'Something is bothering you, Vijay. I can make out from your eyes', Radha said, looking in my eyes. She could sense my eyes were tired and telling her that I was disturbed.

'I don't know, Radha. I think there is something wrong with me and if this continues, I might go insane.'

'Tell me, Vijay. Don't worry, just go ahead', Radha said, placing her hand gently on mine.

'You know about Mrs. Castellino?'

'That old lady, who lived at Summer Hall Cottage?'

'Yes, that same lady', I nodded.

'What about her?'

'I think her ghost is haunting me.'

'Why? There has to be a reason.' Radha believed what I said. She patiently heard me out.

'You know, when Philip died his eyes were searching for me. I am a coward, Radha. Philip tried to save Ballu, that same Ballu who was against Philip. Philip was a far better person than me in many ways. Courage was just one of them.' I took a long pause as I started choking on my words.

'Control yourself, Vijay. Just speak out', Radha pressed my hand, reassuring me.

'I am a coward, Radha. I should have tried to save Philip. He was bleeding. The second mistake I made was with Mrs. Castellino.'

'What has Mrs. Castellino's death got to do with you, Vijay?'

'The day before Mrs. Castellino died I went in to inquire about her. She was sobbing in pain and had high fever. She requested me to call the doctor but due to my carelessness I never managed to call the doctor. By the time doctor reached, it was too late. Mrs. Castellino had died.'

'Don't think about it, Vijay. It's just a sense of guilt in you. Believe me, it was not your fault. Just don't think about it.'

'No, Radha. Every time I pass by her bungalow, I can clearly hear her sobbing cries. It's difficult, Radha. You won't believe it but she is haunting me.'

'Are you sure?' Radha asked.

'Believe me, Radha. I would never lie to you.'

'Come with me', Radha got up and pulled my hand.

'But where are we going?'

'We will see what is there in Mrs. Castellino's bungalow.'

We went on Camel's Back Road and then headed towards the bungalow.

'Can you hear it, Radha? I can hear clearly', I said holding firmly on to Radha's hand.

'Are you sure these are the same sobbing cries that you told me about?'

'I'm absolutely sure, Radha, I cannot be mistaken. I hear them day and night.'

'Come, let's check them.'

'No, Radha. It's unsafe inside.'

'Don't worry, Vijay. I'm with you', Radha pulled my hand and took me towards the bungalow.

We walked along the gravel-filled pathway and entered the garden. The front-door was locked. The nameplate of Mrs. Castellino still hung on one side of the door while the other side another board proclaimed the name of the cottage in bold 'Summer Hall Cottage'. Radha broke one of the windowpanes and unlatched the window. She jumped in and instructed me to follow her inside the house.

The sobbing cries were now more clear and rampant. Radha followed those cries, holding my hand firmly. She tried to concentrate trying to find the direction. Was it the lobby or the bedroom? Radha followed, her footsteps leading us towards the kitchen. In one corner of the kitchen lay a big carton. Radha knew the cries were generating from that carton.

'That's what it is, Vijay', Radha said, pointing towards the carton.

'What is it?' I was a bit confused.

'Go and check it out, yourself', Radha said.

Slowly, I came near the carton and tried to look inside. Suddenly, a big black cat jumped out of the carton and ran towards the lobby. My heart was almost in my mouth. I slowly peeped inside the carton; inside the carton were four little kittens, crying. I succumbed to the floor resting against the wall. My heart was beating violently and knees shivering, I took a deep breath and gently took those little kittens in my arm.

'So these little devils were haunting you', Radha said, taking one of the kittens in her arm.

'They sounded like sobbing cries.'

'I knew they were cries of kittens, but I wanted you to clear this image from your mind. What has happened to you, Vijay? Mrs Castellino died two years ago! For God's sake, come to your senses!' Radha almost burst into bout of tears.

'We have to fight, Vijay. I'm with you. I have already lost Philip and I cannot afford to lose you', Radha held my hand assuring me. I knew that if Radha was with me, I could fight for everything, even myself.

'Oh, Radha. Never leave me. You are my strength and you are everything I have.' I buried my head in her arms and her arms cradled my neck. We held each other like that for some time.

'Don't worry, Vijay. I'm always there for you', Radha said, running her fingers through my hair. There had never been any sign of exceptional passion between us but it seemed like Radha felt much more intense love for me today. This love was more protective and caring than intimate and sexual. I thought to myself, *everything happens for a reason.* I understood the reason now. Radha was made for me and God had granted me my love. No one would ever come between us anymore.

Eleven

'Depression is the most common type of brain disorder in most parts of the world. The clinical picture is dominated by relatively stable, often paranoid delusions, usually accompanied by hallucinations, particularly of the auditory variety, and perceptual disturbances. Disturbances of affect, volition, and speech, and catatonic symptoms are not prominent', Doctor Kakar gave his opinion after giving me a patient hearing.

'Doctor, these voices are common. At times, I hear my grandpa. Initially I thought it was natural because he had been with me since I was born. At times, I hear Philip whistling and humming, and now Mrs Castellino, who died two years ago.'

'Are you on drugs or consume alcohol?' asked the doctor.

'No sir, never.'

'Then the problem lies in your brain.'

I looked at Radha, confused about what could be wrong with my brain.

'At times, we think we are completely in control of our brain, but the brain can sneak out', Dr Kakar explained.

'The brain is never at rest and is always manipulating your emotions; it is affecting how you feel and how you respond to those feelings. The amygdala, which is part of the limbic system, is associated with the fear reaction. A person may, at times, report an intense feeling of fear or danger, which at times may lead to hallucinations.'

I nodded, trying to understand the problem, but these terms were scientific and I had no clue about my brain except that it had some major problem.

'Common symptoms include feeling body sensations such as crawling or other skin sensations. Others are hearing sounds and voices, seeing patterns of light or smelling foul odours. The cause may be drugs, high fever or a threatening feeling.

'Hallucinatory voices that threaten the patient or give commands, or auditory hallucinations without verbal form, such as whistling, humming or laughing are symptoms of the kind of disorder that I can associate with your mental disorder', he explained.

'Feeling of guilt can also be a cause?' I asked.

'Yes. A strong feeling of guilt and self-pitying, particularly criticising oneself for some fault perceived may also be a cause.'

'Can I be cured, Doctor?'

'These conditions are peculiar to people who have a genetic history. Counseling does help but ultimately, you must understand that it starts in your mind and if you have the strength to control your mind, you can definitely win over it.'

'Doctor, I want an honest answer – do I have to live with it or is there a way out?'

'There are some drugs available, which help only to suppress your condition. The cure only depends on how you take things from here. However, John Nash, the famous mathematician and Noble Laureate is one great example who regained his grip on paranoid schizophrenia, without the use of medications after a very long time of psychosis. That was the extreme case and what your case seems is just an initial stage. Studies indicate that the first episode treatment can greatly improve recovery and untreated problems can make things worse.'

I looked at Radha; she knew my eyes were searching for strength in her. We left the hospital but I was still thinking about what Dr Kakar had said about a family history affecting this kind of disorder. My father was an alcoholic; maybe he had symptoms. Grandpa too, had had a paralytic attack. Does that prove something? I was unsure if I would have to live with ghosts haunting me day and night. I didn't know how to fight my own illusions which my mind had created. Should I lock myself inside my house forever or roam around the streets like a crazy man?

Radha sensed my fears, she held my hand, reassuring me that things would be okay, to not give in without a fight.

I didn't know whether I was suffering from a disease, or was it my mental weakness? Was it the pain of losing Grandpa or was I carrying the guilt of Philip's death? I didn't know the answers to my questions; the only fact I knew was that I'd been living with ghosts for almost six months now. After the episode with Mrs. Castellino, I would hear every sound with utmost care. At times, the tick-tock of the wall clock sounded like blood dripping on the floor from the ceiling, the cries of jackals sounded like a hundred people crying aloud outside my door. The whistling of the wind sounded like thunderstorm. At night, I would close my eyes and try to sleep, but I was afraid of the dark. When I switched on the lights, the shadows haunted me. The minutes seems like ages. During the day, people haunted me. They appeared to me as policemen in disguise, on the lookout for me; they know I'm Philip's friend and they would shoot me one day. I wanted to shut all the doors and lock myself inside so that no one would be able to find me. I knew I must make an underground bunker for myself to hide in; that would be a good idea. At times felt like hanging myself from the ceiling fan, or slashing my wrist and watch the blood ooze out slowly. It felt like it would be less painful to see my blood ooze out, drop by drop, until my body was pale and white rather than live with all these ghosts haunting me.

While going through this struggle, I would think about Radha; her words lingering on my mind:

'I've lost Philip; I cannot afford to lose you. Fear, panic, terror, these three words are nothing just a limited thoughts in your mind. If you want to find light, tread into the darkness, do the things that you are afraid of and your fears will be afraid of you.'

To keep myself sane, I would say these things to myself. I repeated what Radha said to me, a hundred times, like a child. I have to fight, I must fight. I will fight all my fears, I will fight myself. If not for the world, if not even for myself, I will for the one I love, for Radha. I fought and fought hard. It is easy to fight the whole world, but it's difficult to fight yourself and even more difficult to fight your own shadows, your thoughts and your fears. Every time these negative thoughts lingered on my mind, I thought about Radha. Whenever the dark and unknown voices echoed to haunt me, I thought about the sweet voice of Radha. When the daunting, dark shadows overpowered me, I remembered

Radha's face and the ray of hope behind her smile. Radha was my strength, she was my hope; she was not in my prayers, she *was* my prayer. She helped me come out of this darkness; she was a ray of hope for me. She was what I discovered as the greatest strength around, she was love.

My mission and reason to live was only one name now – Radha. If in my wildest dreams I had the chance to win her, then I must find a platform, a firm ground for myself where we would build a new hope from the shades of love and colours of my dreams. From that day onwards, I was on the lookout for a suitable job. I applied for all competitive exams I could lay my hands on. I applied for all kinds of exams – civil services, police services, banking, clerical, hotel management; I filled all available forms. After serious preparing for six months, I cleared the Combined Defense Services exam. I appeared for my interview, cleared it and also managed to clear the medicals. I do believe that destiny is fixed and there is a reason for every damn thing that happens around us. Everything has a reason behind it, a purpose, big or small, good or bad. I was destined to wear this olive green uniform and things happened automatically. Otherwise, my history of depression would have come to light during the medical board. Before I could realise anything, the joining instructions were in my hand.

Knock… knock!

'Who's there?'

Knock…knock! This time I knocked a bit harder.

'Wait a minute, I'm coming', Radha opened the door.

'Vijay, at this hour? Is everything all right?' Radha asked, looking a bit surprised to see me on her doorstep after dark.

'I've come to show you something', I pulled out the joining letter from my pocket and waggled it in front of Radha.

'What is this?'

'I'm going to Doon. My training at the Indian Military Academy starts from Monday.'

'That's wonderful! So when are you leaving?'

'Tomorrow morning. I know it would not be possible to meet you early in the morning, so I decided to see you now.'

'That's alright, Vijay. Good luck.'

'Radha, there is something important I want to discuss with you. Can you be with me tonight? There are so many things I want to discuss with you.'

'Okay, but I will have to come back soon.'

I had made all the arrangements – good food, chocolate pudding and juice. I placed a few candles on the center table with a couple of chairs to make things look a bit romantic. I poured some juice for myself and prepared a glass for Radha.

'Vijay, you wanted to say something?'

I was still wondering about how to go about it. After a deep breath and gathering all my confidence, I said, 'Radha, if someone proposed to you for marriage, what would be your reply?' Radha looked awestruck. She kept quiet she didn't respond.

Witnessing her silence over the issue, I asked her again.

'Radha, I mean if someone wants to marry you and he proposes to you, what would be your reply?'

'It depends on who has asked the question.'

'If Philip was here at this moment and had proposed to you, what would have been your answer?' Radha looked at me when I mentioned Philip's name, and then looked down in embarrassment. Tears seemed to have filled her eyes.

'V-Vijay, my dad will be back any moment. I should leave', Radha said in trembling voice and stood up to go. I held her hand.

'Radha, I know you loved Philip and I wouldn't have asked you if he was here with us.'

'Vijay, Philip will always be with us. I can feel him within me.' Her voice was trembling and she was almost crying now.

'I know your feelings, Radha but you cannot live with a ghost forever. Marry me, Radha.'

After complete silence, I repeated my words.

'I love you, Radha. Marry me.'

'I don't know, Vijay, how to react, what to say.'

'Okay, tell me one thing, do you love me?'

Radha was silent, a stream of tears flowing from her eyes.

'Answer me, Radha. Do you love me?' I wanted to hug her, kiss her, but held back.

'Radha, just wait for a few more days and I will be back to take you with me forever.' Radha was still silent. I understood she didn't want to discuss the issue any further. We quietly had dinner. After we finished, I went to the kitchen to get the chocolate pudding.

Radha was tired and sleepy, her eyes started to close. Soon, we finished our pudding but now it was difficult for Radha to keep herself awake. I carried her to the bed. For once, she looked at me and then gently closed her eyes. I looked at her, how beautiful she was and I knew that in a few hours I will be away from her, I didn't even know for how long. I wanted to look at her sleep like that forever.

When I woke up, it was four in the morning. I knew it was time for Radha to go home before her Dad woke up. I accompanied her till the beginning of the alley near her house. As she was about to leave I asked her, 'Radha, remember what I asked you? Marry me, Radha.'

'Vijay, I will always pray for your success, wherever you are. Good luck, Vijay, you have a new world in front of you now.' She waved her hand, but I didn't have the courage to look in her eyes anymore or say goodbye to her. She moved on and she was soon invisible in the darkness. I was not sure if this was the last time we were together but within my heart I knew I had lost her.

My voice started to tremble. I wanted to speak but I was unable to say anything.

'Vijay, keep telling your story.'

'Sir, his pulse is going down. I think we are losing him.'

'Vijay, fight on! We have almost reached. Just hang on... You cannot leave at the —

Part Two

Twelve

'Wonderful to see you recover so soon, Vijay. In just over a month!' Doctor Shahid was examining my reports.

'Doctor, I am planning to quit the Army.'

'Okay. Do you have some other avenues outside?'

'I don't know but I cannot be a liability on the Army. I think I should explore my fortune outside', I said in a faint voice. I knew I was downgraded to low medical category. I had a perforation in my liver and two vertebrae discs had been damaged, which had been removed post surgery.

'Hey, I just remembered. That day, you were telling me your story, I must say I was quite curious to know further. Come over for a cup of coffee this evening. We can also look over the documentation required for per-mature retirement on medical grounds.'

'Definitely, sir, see you in the evening.'

If my Grandpa had taught me what life was and had made me a human being, the Army taught me the art of survival and had made me a warrior. My mind was nurtured by my grandpa's teachings and it was toughened by military training. One and a half years of rigorous training had converted a weak boy named Vijay into a rugged, disciplined and fearless soldier, Lieutenant Vijay Amrit Raj Sharma. The Army taught me what team spirit meant; it taught me how to fight even when you have no life left in you. It is the never say die attitude that was imbibed in me.

"Fight with your hands if you don't have a weapon, fight with your feet if your hands are broken. Bite with your teeth if your feet are cut, and fight with your soul if there is no life left in your body."

After training, I was granted two weeks' leave cum joining time. I moved back to Mussoorie only for my love, Radha. I had a million dreams in my eyes for a new life and a new beginning. But life had some other plans for me.

I met Radha's dad, I had made up my mind that I would ask for Radha's hand. But Radha was not there; one and a half years is a long time and in fact, Radha was already a married woman. It's true – *time and tide wait for none.* She was married to a software engineer from Meerut. It had been four months that she was married and was living a happy married life. Somewhere I had the feeling that Radha's dad knew that I had come to ask for Radha's hand. However, he never said anything except that she was married, her husband was working in Bangalore and she was also in Bangalore. He also told me that Radha was very happy now.

Time is a very big player in all spheres of this universe and I knew it was time for us to say goodbye forever. Time – what exactly is it? Was there a time when time was born? Can we go back in time and bring back Philip and our days? Or does time flow like emotions? Or like tears? Time makes us live with dreams in our eyes, and then it shatters everything. Once again it was showing me a path but an unknown one. Love has many forms and I understood what love meant. I don't understand relationships; relationships will definitely destroy me. Time is harsh; it is cruel. However, time is friendship and it leaves behind memories to linger on your mind forever. Time flies like a flock of birds – you want to capture it but it is too fast to be trapped. There was time of love, of friendship. There is time where every passing moment seems like ages; you want to run away but it's a trap. I don't know if time is an angel or a demon but yes it has all the power of the universe. I don't know after losing the purpose of my life how my life will turn out? But definitely, Vijay Amrit Raj will move on. I love Radha and if again time conspires to unite us then I will definitely meet her before I die. But right now, I have to move on, specially Vijay Amrit Raj who has some purpose to fulfill and that will be my salvation. I will surely pray for Radha every day and night, wherever I am and in whatever I do.

We all feel that the life we live is not the one chosen by us, but circumstances have forced us to go some other way. I wanted to be a writer but I was destined to join the Army. I wanted to marry Radha but her destiny too was fixed. It's the same story with almost all of us. The bank manager wanted to be a cricketer, the housewife aspires to become a model. How do we decide what we want? It is all controlled by our brain. Beauty attracts our mind and our body responds to it. It gives you joy. The path where we want to travel is made by our aspirations and desire, of dreams and imagination, in search of joy. All these scientific theories may be proven to be true, but today also I feel the same, no matter whatever destiny has in store, Radha was my strength, she was my love and in my lonely thoughts, she was there to fill in the vacuum of my life.

I tried to run in different directions while searching for so many things. I ran in search of friendship but Philip was gone. I tried to regain my strength to follow my grandpa's footsteps but Grandpa was hidden in God's lap. I know he was God's favorite disciple. I wandered along a lonely path to discover love, but Radha was nowhere. I wandered like a cloud unable to decide which way to go. I asked God what He wanted. Why me? If nothing else, at least show me the way. All doors cannot be closed for me. Then a voice within me replied. I could hear grandpa speaking to me.

"Why are you running in different directions? What are you searching for? When there is nothing at all, now on from this nothing your world starts? Don't worry, my child. Just hold my finger in a new world. There won't be any sorrows for you because the meaning of joy itself is lost. There won't be any pain because pleasure itself has no meaning. There won't be hope because despair is an unknown word. From here on a new journey begins a new life in search of true knowledge, in the line of duty to our motherland."

I learned the essence of life after wandering like a vagrant cloud that *the path is the way*, so follow the path shown by God, he will lead to your true destiny. Yes, the destination is the journey itself. *The Path is the way*.

January 1999, a new year and a new beginning; my battalion was my new home. The twelfth battalion of the elite Rajputana Rifles, my new identity: Lieutenant Vijay Amrit Raj Sharma, and my new postal address from now onwards: C/O 56 APO (care of 56 Army Post Office).

My battalion was deployed on the line of control (LOC), a battle zone without rules, without border pillars and no sanctity of boundaries. I was sent at the forward post, all I had in my possession were a few bunkers to protect myself and my men from enemy artillery shelling, the enemy within eyeball contact constantly gazing towards me and my strength; my platoon of 30 valiant soldiers. The day I reached I was briefed in detail by the platoon JCO Subedar Bhawar Singh, a six feet three inches tall and strong man from Jodhpur, Rajasthan. He told me the laws of the LOC: rule no. one – there are no rules of engagement; we get a chance to shoot them, shoot without hesitation, because if they will get a chance they will shoot us. Rule no. two – the importance of camouflage; do not be visible or do not move outside the bunker, move only when it is dark, and the most important rule: there are no rules for either of the teams.

The area familiarisation of my post and understanding the positions of adversaries was hardly over when the true feel of the LOC was revealed to me. I remember, I was at the view point, just thirty meters away from my bunker when a *buzz....!* hissed passed me and within a second, a blast behind me took me aback. The sentry from the nearby bunker shouted, *'Saab*! Take cover! Enemy artillery shelling has started!'* Within no time I realised the peril to my life and I rushed to my bunker.

We had all cuddled inside our bunkers, under the thuds of roaring blasts and splinters flying all around. After about an hour, the shelling stopped and before we could regain our positions, the enemy automatics and direct firing weapons opened up. I was furious as to why our men were not giving them a befitting reply. After all, we were under intense artillery shelling and now automatics. I could not believe that we were here only to duck down and hide inside our bunkers. After the firing stopped, I called the senior JCO and asked him about why we were not replying to them? He just told me that it wasn't the right time.

Then, at midnight, I was again taken aback by the familiar loud thud. This time, it was our artillery pounding on the enemy post right in front of me. The roar once again lasted for about an hour, unless it was over for the day. The same drill continued with altered timings. I felt it a bit absurd – firing at each other without a reason and wasting precious ammunition. I decided to meet the post commander of the adversaries. I requested for a flag meeting. The officer was Captain Rahman Akthar, I told him no point firing at each other, and we mutually agreed to avoid firing and live peacefully. He agreed and was happy and appreciated my concern over the issue. The next three months there was absolute peace, at least in the area of the LOC where I was deployed.

Then in the month of May, when I was about to go on leave and was thinking about a well-deserved break, things changed. There was news of enemy intrusion in the Kargil sector. All leaves were canceled and those currently on leave were called back. Our battalion was earmarked to prepare for offensive in the sector. The deadlock between Captain Rahman Akthar and me also broke and the same drill of Artillery shelling started again, this time with vengeance.

Those were the days when everybody was talking about Kargil war, indeed everyone at that point of time wanted to be at the war front. In the first week of May, the confirmation of intrusion was authenticated beyond doubt. By mid-May, the Indian Army retaliated but it was difficult fighting in high altitudes and barren lands without cover. We all felt miserable because it's a soldier's dream and duty to fight for the nation, which was the reason we existed.

First it was the success of second battalion The Rajputana Rifles who captured three pimple and Tololing to prove that nothing is impossible. After the initial success, finally, on June 29 we captured two vital posts – point 5060 and point 5100 near Tiger Hill. By July 14, the then Prime Minister, Mr Atal Bihari Vajpayee declared Operation Vijay a success. I was proud of the fact that the operation was called Vijay. The Indian Army once again proved its mettle and proved to the world that even the most invincible peaks of Kargil were not impossible. I was a bit disappointed for not getting a chance to participate in the war but at the same time I was a proud soldier of the Indian Army.

The Kargil conflict had brought us face to face with loss of vital territory, nuclear blackmail and possible national dishonor. The grave situation could only be retrieved by selfless gallantry of our young officers and soldiers. Under this tricolor we live and we came back after waving the tricolor on those invincible peaks or we came back wrapped in it. *Jai Hind*. Every damn thing has a price and for our victory we gave away 527 lives and 1363 were wounded.

The new millennium brought vibrant and dynamic changes across the world. The struggle that had taken Philip's life finally gave new hope to many in the form of a new hill state. Uttranchal was the new state declared. Apart from this, a new revolution had gripped the world in its claws, called the IT revolution. Cell phones were now a reality and affordable to the masses; incoming calls on mobiles became free of cost. Electronics, two wheelers, cars and other gadgets that were meant for the elite class, were now as common as the common man. Apart from this, another industry was growing with speed across the world – 'terrorism'.

In September 2001 the 9/11 attacks shook the world. It was the greatest and the most unbelievably coordinated attack, which in future was about to change the face of the entire world. Soon in December, same year the democratic symbol of India was attacked. If 9/11 changed the face of the world then the parliament attacks changed the equilibrium of the armed forces. Earlier we all had a balanced profile of peace – field – peace postings, which now suddenly changed to field – field – field. My unit was deployed in Dalhousie peace station after its grueling tenure of north-east. Then it was deployed on LOC due to Kargil debacle. Then in June 2001, we received orders to move to peace location in Jaipur, which was amended as deployment on border in Jaisalmer sector post parliament attack. We were ready with our defenses along the border, waiting for orders to storm in and kept waiting for almost a year, after which we were ordered to move back in December 2002.

With our unit move order, there was another posting order. This one was for me. I was posted to Rashtriya Rifles and within a month I was to report to my new battalion located in J&K in the Surankote sector. I moved on with the enlightened motto in life... *The Path is the Way.*

Thirteen

January 2004: a new day, a new month and a new year; cold, chilly, and intoxicating. Cold feelings and cold weather mesmerise me. All I want to do is cuddle inside the quilt with a hot cup of tea in my bunker and relive the good old days thinking about Mussoorie, Grandpa, Philip, and Radha. I sit beside a small kerosene stove trying to get some life back in my fingers and toes. Everything out here is cold like me; no warmth, neither in my room nor inside me. I try to read a book I have been trying to finish but I find myself more engrossed in my own thoughts. I keep the book aside and think about the patrol party that has been out since morning, a bit worried about why they were not back. I slowly sip my tea and put on some music; I find it a little boring since I've been listening to these songs day after day, again and again. This loneliness, I know, will kill me one day; it's been a part of my life for quite some time now but it still haunts me. There is nothing worse than the feeling of no one caring whether I exist or what I have to say about life. I know the world will continue to turn without my awkward presence. To live all by yourself, you either have to be a ghost or God.

I know it is important to let my past go. I want to release myself from this cage, and that is the reason why I am moving on. I step outside and try to see God in nature, in the snow on the mountains and in the valley. The colour of the earth is white here, white full of snow; the leaves, rooftops, vehicles, lawns all covered with white flakes of snow. *I ask myself isn't this beautiful? If it is, then why I am gloomy?* Everything is pure like this snow. All are delighted, the birds, men, mountains, rivers. They smile and admire this purity blessed upon them from the heavens above, they smile upon it and capture every moment of bliss. The sunshine reflects the fresh snow on the mountain; the newborn stream finds its way between the mountain curves in search of its journey, reminding me of something. Remember, *the path is the way.*

The mountain in the horizon glistens with the sun reflecting on the snow. I look up to the blue sky and let the rays of the sun fall on my face. I close my eyes and feel the warmth; a pleasing sensation traveling from my face to my spine and my soul. I open my eyes and smile at the heavens above. I am indeed thankful and pray quietly, listening to the voices of nature. The faint giggling of the Suran River between the valley, the chirping of birds and sometimes unseen but always heard in my heart: the voice of Radha. Invisible words manifest itself in this visible world.

Once more, I look at the blue sky above, this time Radha on my mind. I ask the blue sky the questions I used to ask Grandpa when I was a child.

Why is it hard to forget certain people?

Where did Philip go after he died?

Why are we born if in the end we have to die?

What does God mean?

The mighty Pir Panjal ranges, arrogant and full of pride, respond with the constant sound of wind. I don't know the answer but yes, I'm sure He is replying to me. I have to find these answers and that is the aim of my life. The only thing I know as of now is that I cannot live like a ghost from my past memories. I have to move on and I will find these answers. Yes, *the Path is the Way.*

Time flies like birds in the sky; they are here and in a moment, nowhere. I have completed five years in the Army. Surankote, the majestic valley was my new home. Beneath my post flows the Suran River; the name Surankote emerges from this little river which in due course of time will merge with the mighty Indus River. On the three sides are the visible ranges of Pir Panjal, arrogant, forceful and invincible. The remaining portion is the gentle mother ridge covered with thick Kalaban forest, the play field of all the terrorists, especially the self-styled commander of the Pir Panjal division terrorist group: Abu Ali, our prime target. Abu Ali was the most dreadful and sought after terrorist since the last three years after he massacred thirty-eight people from a single village. Since the last three years we have been trying to hunt him down and now it was my turn to continue the chase.

Eighteen months ago, this particular area was heavily inflicted with terrorist activities. Much before the sun went down, all shops were closed and no vehicle moved on the road after 3pm. The terrorists had nearly taken over this valley. The first and foremost thing that had to be done was winning the lost confidence of people. 'Operation Sadbhavna' was launched with the aim to win the hearts and minds of people and give them their due by showing empathy towards them. Once people had confidence in our cause, they started supporting and helping us. Now it was time to crack down heavily on the terrorists. The only way to do this, I knew, was getting Abu Ali, as that would break the entire terrorist network in the area.

There is a thin line between sloth and greed and what comes out is ambition. Similarly, between secrecy and loquacity lies honesty, and the dividing line between rashness and cowardice is courage. I had none of these qualities to emerge as a leader and a reason for others to follow my footsteps, but I had found a purpose to live and all I could now think about was Abu Ali. It has become an obsession in my mind to get him. Between this entire gambit, one thing I realised was that now I had a purpose, I had a task at hand.

One fine afternoon, just after lunch, I received an intercept. A group of five terrorists were communicating on their satellite phone. They were speaking to 'alpha one', a code named operator across the LOC. It was evident from their conversation that a group of five terrorists were hiding in Kalaban forest and were trying to link up with some guide who would take them across Pir Panjal, which was the dividing line between our area and the Kashmir valley. The code sign of the caller was identified as Uzefa or double seven; I knew it was Abu Ali. The grid references were passed to us and we were ready for action. My company strength was not enough to block all escape routes emerging out of Kalaban forest. The neighboring companies were tasked to block the northern and eastern routes. We left the western route free because it led back to the LOC fence and the company manning the fence would take care of them. I planked myself at the southern ridge, which was the most evident and preferred route leading to the Pir Panjal.

By the time we were effective with our stops and inner cordon, the sun was already behind the ridge. The canvas of the sky had streaks red. Everyone at the headquarters was panicky. They knew chances for the terrorists to escape in the dark were high. Orders were passed to move in and search the area, it was also emphasised that no collateral damage should take place in the form of civilian casualty. Tensions were already high due to death of one civilian in Sophian village. I knew it was a difficult task so I ordered my specialist men or *ghataks* under *Havildar* Dharampal to search the area.

We moved cautiously, trying to figure out any trails; no traces were evident and as it was getting dark we were losing our confidence of getting any telltale signs. As we approached the dry riverbed running midway dividing the Kalaban forest into two halves, a loud thud brought us down and we started running for cover. Then, a few more loud bursts; I knew rifle grenades were fired on us. Only Dharampal was able to locate the small knoll from which we were under fire. He retaliated and then there was a series of exchange of continuous fire. Soon, the terrorists moved behind the knoll. Between all this firefight, the scout, Birender, was injured. He was wearing a bulletproof jacket but the flying splinters of the air burst rifle grenade had penetrated his neck. He was bleeding profusely and it became a challenge to evacuate him. I took a decision to fall back, going behind them would have been foolish and we would have bought more casualties. I knew the hiding terrorists had many visible targets to pin down and we had only speculations and invisible targets to locate; guerrilla warfare is definitely a risky preposition for the armed forces. But Dharampal was confident of knocking down one of them, I know he rarely misses the target.

We moved back to our previous location, at the mule track emerging out of the dark forest. On stretcher-bearers, Birender was evacuated but I knew his body was cold and lifeless before we reached the periphery of the forest. I kept quiet; losing a man would definitely affect the morale of others. Now it was time to wait for the night to get over to continue with the search at first light, I knew this night would be a long one.

Then, at half past three in the night, sounds of firing made our senses alert. I could make out there was some contact going on at the northern ridge, probably at the junction point where two seasonal streams merged. I prayed that the contact was a successful one but the sequence of firing gave me a hint that the terrorists had probably escaped. Initially, there was an AK burst fired, which was continuous and seemed as if the trigger was pulled until the entire magazine was empty. Then, we heard indiscriminate firing of Light Machine Gun (LMG) as if they were trying to shoot in the dark. One-minute later illumination round was fired to light up the area and a few shots in the dark were heard. I could analyse that terrorists were trying to escape after bumping into one of our stops; they fired and fled and before our men could retaliate, they had escaped.

Four terrorists were moving down from the dry stream and the alert sentry had tracked their movement with the help of Night Vision Device (NVD). He informed his officer – a newly commissioned officer – Lieutenant Pandey. The young officer was not sure if they were civilians or terrorists. As they came close, Lieutenant Pandey challenged them and they answered with their Kalashnikov rifles. Pandey was seriously injured and the terrorists jumped on the other side in the gorge.

The next morning, the search began as four columns of a platoon size were launched to comb the entire area. Two dead bodies were found, one from the knoll where we had our initial contact and a second in the dry riverbed where

Lieutenant Pandey had been injured. I knew three of them had escaped and we would get nothing. The higher officials still hoped to get something and for three days it was jungle bashing in rain or sun, without changing our clothes or shoes and without any sleep. It was only on the fourth morning that the operation was called off. Lieutenant Pandey suffered a critical injury in his right leg; four complete round bursts had hit him below the right knee because of which his right leg was amputated. I felt sorry for the young lieutenant – at the age of twenty-three, the young officer had lost his limb but I'm sure he would be proud to display it as a wound suffered for the motherland; he must feel proud of himself.

Abu Ali was giving us sleepless nights especially after the Kalaban operation, which had emerged as the Achilles heel for the Army. Although we had killed two terrorists, three had managed to escape. We'd lost one of our men and one officer had been critically injured. Abu Ali was present somewhere around – in my area of responsibility – and we had concrete information about it. All hopes were on my battalion to get him and my battalion had faith in my company and me. I had put all my money on Manzoor, a SOG member. Manzoor was a surrendered militant who had been with Abu Ali, but when the minority massacre had taken place Manzoor realised it was not a freedom struggle but a devilish act and he had surrendered himself. Manzoor advised me to reduce all operations for some time and let Abu Ali be complacent. We did exactly the same and after two months of patience, Manzoor got us the vital information. I realised it is not the strength or the weapons but the patience that gets one his prey. I had waited and then that eventful night came when we got Abu Ali. It was during that same operation where I was injured.

Fourteen

One thing that life has always tried to teach me is to move on. Like the river, life flows on and we should also flow with the current; where we are heading should not be the concern. Complete the circle; the aim should be clear in mind and that is more important than any other thing. I got the chance to serve in the Army, maybe I was destined to bring Abu Ali to justice but my injuries would not allow me to serve further in the Army with pride, and so I decided to seek a fortune somewhere else. My wounds gained me a gallantry award but made me a liability on the Army. I understood His command and I decided to leave the Army and search for whatever else was waiting for me.

The Army resettlement course gave me an opportunity to do a management course from Indian Institute of Management (IIM). Soon after hanging my uniform, I was employed in a multinational firm located in Bangalore. Days, weeks, months and years passed by. I now had enough money in my bank account to buy a three-bedroom flat in Bangalore. I had a house, a car, and everything that money could buy but emptiness still prevailed inside me. I knew what my life was missing – a life partner, my Grandfather and most importantly, a friend like Philip. Whenever I would think about love, Radha was the name that lingered on my mind. I knew Radha was just a word now, a mere thought in my heart and mind, just a pain, a sorrow, my loneliness, my weakness yet my strength. It was the name that brought a smile on my face and tears in my eyes. How incomplete my life was without her, yet complete in my own world of fantasy.

On weekdays I was busy with my routine of going to office, attending meetings, completing tasks at hand and when I came back to my haunted apartment, two large drinks of scotch followed by dinner laid on the table by my maid and that was enough for me to call it a day. The difficult part was spending weekends where I had nothing to do and that's when the illusions of my past and Radha made me restless. The more I tried to run away from them, the more they chased me. I decided to search for a new reason to live, to kill time and avert my loneliness. Clubs, cafés, movies, bars, alcohol, these were perfect for forgetting anything and everything. I could think of nothing else but Radha and I cannot even completely convey the intolerable wretchedness of my separation from her. I tried to fill all my days with appointments and duties and it still did not save me in the least from a lonely emptiness.

The worst part was that I didn't know what I'd been searching for all these days on dark, desolate, lonely nights and forlorn roads. Am I searching for my penance so that my mind is free from the cage named Radha? Or am I in need of a partner where I may find some love and a reason to live? I knew I had become lifeless. After lots of introspection I knew it was only Radha who could revive the life in me and I decided to search for her. I inquired everywhere – in Mussoorie, asked old friends and relatives and then finally, I found her. I learnt that she was in San Francisco, USA. I had already made up my mind to go there. I knew we had our company's office in San Francisco as well and I requested the management to send me there. The management had inhibitions about sending me to San Francisco but when I threatened to quit my job, they agreed to send me for a month to finish a few pending projects and then depending on the developments they would decide on the future.

Before boarding my British Airways flight, I sent an email to Radha; I had managed to get her email ID from one of her old college friends. One thing technology had granted us was that it was not difficult to track anyone. I just dropped a simple mail stating that I was coming to San Francisco for some work and that I came to know that she was there so if she could share her address and number with me. During the entire nine-hour journey to Heathrow Airport London, where I had to change my flight for San Francisco I kept thinking about whether I would get any response from her or not. In case I don't, all my efforts will go to waste. Then, after security check at Heathrow airport, I got couple of hours to check my mails. Yes there was a mail from Radha – it was a regular mail inquiring about my whereabouts for all these years. She gave me her address and number. She was staying in San Jose. I immediately booked a hotel room in San Jose near her apartment and canceled the one that had already been booked by my company. I knew the next twelve-hour journey would be restless and I could see a smile on my face after a long time. I kept thinking about Radha until the flight landed in San Francisco.

San Francisco is one of the world's principal banking and finance centers; a pioneer in making banking services accessible to the middle class. Many large financial institutions, multinational banks and venture capital firms are based in or have regional headquarters in the city. With over 30 international financial institutions, companies, and a large support infrastructure of professional services including law, public relations and design. San Francisco is designated as one of the top twenty global financial centers. Since a decade, San Francisco's economy has increasingly been tied to India, sharing the need of highly educated workers with IT skills. It was my turn to explore the city but I was not there to find a new fortune in the IT sector. I knew why I was here – Radha.

The same evening I called Radha from the hotel room. She sounded dim but also invited me home for dinner. I knew it was after a very long time I will be seeing her. I had no idea how I would react, I had no idea what we would say, it seemed like an age had passed by and God had brought me back to her so that I could find my redemption. I bought a bottle of wine and a bunch of roses for her. I knew she was married so I was preparing myself to react in a very normal manner although there were undercurrents swinging in my heart and mind.

My heart began to beat aloud as I approached her apartment door. Apartment no. 123, I reconfirmed and then with a little hesitation I knocked the door. After a few seconds the door opened and Radha stood before me wearing a pair of pink trousers and a blue T-shirt. Her face looked up at me, her eyes deep yet displaying pain and tenderness and resignation. In her face, I could see suffering that was growing old, as if because we were left on our self and accepted our destiny and it seemed this wound will never heal. I could see in her face the same expression that I had seen years ago when I had asked her to marry me; she was cold, unmoved, without any touch of feelings. She gave a faded smile as our eyes met for a brief moment before I looked down in embarrassment.

'Hi Vijay, good to see you after so many years', she said, and let me in.

'Welcome, sir, welcome... I am Shyam Kumar, Radha's husband.'

'It's a pleasure meeting you, sir', I greeted him with a fake smile and for a moment thought about why on earth would Radha decide to marry such a person. He was older than her by about ten years, his major portion of head was bald and remaining had majority strands of white shades. Another thing I knew was that he was a divorcée, then why did Radha decide to marry him? I felt really bad and my decision to win back Radha became even firmer.

At the dinner table, Shyam did most of the talking, just casual conversation. At intervals, I glanced at Radha. Our eyes would meet for a brief moment until we both looked down. There were so many things I wanted to say to Radha, I wanted to tell her I was here because I was selfish and I needed her so that I could live, as selfishly as my lungs breathe air. I needed her in my life so that I could live, this was the only way I could love; I was surrendering myself completely at her mercy.

After dinner we continued with our casual conversation until I decided to say goodbye and informed them that I was staying at a hotel just a street away. Shyam told me to live with them; he knew Radha and I were college friends but I knew I would never be able to live with them. I could never stand anyone sharing the same bed with Radha, even if that person was her husband.

For several days, I thought I should call on Radha. I had no idea what to say, but felt dimly that I should say something to make her understand that I was there to take her with me. Often, Shyam would invite me for a drink or dinner but I kept putting it off even though I did not have much work to do and had lots of spare time for myself. I moved from one place to another in San Francisco, trying to find a place where I could find peace, where I could find myself. While I negotiated my way through the dense, bustling city, I admired the picturesque skyline, the hills and Victorians. All I could see were cranes, buildings and high-rise condos. No doubt San Francisco is a beautiful city, the poets and artists have been singing its praises ever since it was created. The best part of the city is its geographical location on the pacific coast.

I wandered all alone, trying to find a new world or maybe I was trying to find my own share of the world, trying to figure out how to steal it for myself. At sunset, I would be all alone at the Golden Gate Bridge, lost in my thoughts, only to make myself believe even more that I would be able to impress Radha and take her away with me. At times, I would wander, all alone, at Pier 39 – watching a lonely ship at the horizon, revealing my own loneliness at heart. I went from one place to other – North Beach, Chinatown but nothing would attract me. Was this city like a capricious woman taking too much time to seduce me? My visit to Alcatraz, the old military prison gave me chills and cold sweats. Was my conscience bothering me? I felt like a criminal witnessing those walls and after that I never tried to explore new places.

Then, during one of the weekends, I dropped in for dinner at Radha's house. It was a carefree Saturday evening and we sat together in the balcony and drank beer. I told Shyam my favorite tale about how I got hold of the most wanted terrorist, Abu Ali, when I was in the Army. I boasted in detail about my solitary tale of bravado and about my injuries – liver perforation and damaged vertebrae discs. Shyam was an expert software programmer, but his IT stories were not at all interesting, but when he told me how he happened to meet Radha all my senses were alert. He told me that Radha was working under him; he was her team leader. Because he was ten years elder to Radha, he never ever thought that Radha would fall in love with him. Indeed, Shyam never had any kind of affection for Radha until the day when Radha proposed him for marriage.

'Was this your second marriage?' I knew the answer and yet, I wanted to hear this from him. At times, pinching someone at his wounds gives you immense pleasure, a short bout of victory, and I was fighting to steal his wife.

'I'm sorry I really don't know if it is the right question to ask?' I apologized.

'No, Vijay, the truth is the truth and I feel only sad, more for the girl who was forced to marry me, but then I cannot change the truth.' He took a long pause and picked up his glass. I knew something was troubling him, it was the truth and I was glad I asked this question.

'There was someone, her name was Sofia', he said, earnestly sipping his beer. 'The one I loved. She was beautiful, smart, and intelligent but at the same time, ambitious. It was a typical Indian arranged marriage and I had met Sofia only once, and believe me, it was enough to fall in love with her. Then, on the first night of our marriage she asked me something, she asked for divorce.'

'Divorce on first night, was she already having an affair?' I inquired.

'No, not an affair but she had ambition. She refused for marriage, but her parents forced the marriage on to her. She was intelligent and wanted to explore the whole world, and she already had an internship up her sleeve. She wanted to go to Durban for higher studies; marriage was the last thing on her priority.'

'So you divorced her?'

'Love cannot be thrust on anyone and I didn't want to keep someone in a cage just because her parents were unwilling to understand her. I booked her flight tickets for Durban, made all arrangements and subsequently sent her divorce papers.'

That evening after dinner, I took Shyam's permission to leave. I had a pleading look in my eyes when I glanced at Radha's face. Our eyes met, perplexed for an extraordinary moment, then I looked down and for sometime I couldn't look at her again. She said nothing, not even goodbye, I was not sure if she was really happy to see me after so many years or was she repenting her decision to marry Shyam, or was she proud to find such a humble and decent person? I was not sure, but I was sure of one thing - I would take back Radha at any cost.

Fifteen

The vastness and expanse of the universe is unending, at the same time it is unexplored and that is what we call infinity – that which cannot be defined. Infinity starts with an individual; there are countless people in this world and yet we are confined to ourselves. Every individual has his own world and everything in his life revolves around his own solar system in the form of spouse, parents, friends and relatives. Every galaxy in its form has its own priorities and affection. Today, I am in a different world, a different galaxy and I am here because I had chosen to be here. After Philip's death everything had changed, our world had changed; it was like a never-ending eclipse.

I knew Radha was a married woman and I didn't have any rights over her. But her silence haunted me. I knew she wanted to tell me something and if so, why wasn't she saying anything? I don't know if she was really happy with Shyam or she was just living that way because she had found a partner for her needs and companionship. I could feel that Radha was lonely; yes, lonely the way I have been. I could feel that there was no one to care for her, no one to love her and no one to understand how she felt. I wanted to tell her a thousand things, I wanted to know whether she really cared for me, but was difficult to tell a married woman what you were thinking about in your heart and even more difficult to understand what's in her heart. After years, life had brought me at the same crossroads of life where I had to decide to fight for my love or let it go. I knew it would never be easy but then it was Radha – the reason why I was there.

That day, I had put everything at stake for Radha and challenged life to take away everything and grant me just one thing and that was love. So here I am standing and dare to stare in the eyes of God and my destiny to put everything at stake for Radha. I knew that was the place where I would find my redemption. If I have to get over my sins, my cowardice and the reason why Philip died; I have to find myself and find Radha.

Seeing her after so many years made me realise that I had no idea how to behave. I wanted to hug her, kiss her, cry out loud and tell her – look, I've found you and this time I won't let you go at any cost. But to my horror, she was still the same the same incomplete Radha whom I had seen the last time – cold and lifeless. She was without any feelings, I never dared to look in her eyes because they were telling me to go away, she didn't want to even see my face. Eyes are the windows to your soul and I never dared to look in her eyes because I felt scared. Her eyes haunt me; I could see my own reflection in them. Maybe I would have been at ease if she would have shouted at me, cried out loud, told me that she hates me and banged the door on my face. But she never did that and instead, she would meet me every day, wearing a fake smile and would never look into my eyes because she knew there was a devil inside my flesh.

I wanted to say so many things to her but when I looked at her, I became afraid, when I tried to say something, my words shiver and whenever I touch her, her cold body made me feel like I was a sinner. Say something to me, slap me, spit on my face, shout at me, but do something so that I know you are alive. Tell me that I am the worst person one has ever known, but do something so that I know you are alive.

The worst feeling in life is the feeling of being neglected. My conscience will never let me live and I will never get the chance to express myself. She was killing me every day, every moment. I was dying a death every second of my life. Was that not enough vengeance for her? I loved her, I felt for her and that is the reason why I was there. If she'd tell me to go away I would go away forever and I promise I would never show my face to her again, but she only had to say something, her silence was killing me. She had enslaved my soul and only she could set it free.

Time passed by – day after day, minute after minute and then the day came when I had to leave San Francisco. I knew it was now or never and that evening before my flight I went to meet Radha. I looked deep in her eyes for the first time and said,

'Radha, this evening I am leaving for India. I came here only to find you.'

'I know, Vijay, and I am happy that you came so far only for me. Have a safe journey and stay in touch', she replied while looking down. What I was trying to do, I wasn't entirely sure. Was she the Radha who loved Philip, or she was a married Radha who was now dedicated to Shyam? Was she the one whom I loved or the one in whose eyes I had seen hatred for me?

'Radha, come with me. I know you don't love Shyam.'

'Stop it, Vijay.'

'We will find a new world, a life of our dreams and of Philip's soul.' I hugged her and kissed her until she pushed me back.

'Vijay, I am a married woman now.'

'It doesn't make any difference to me.'

'My life is dedicated to Shyam and he is the one for whom I live.'

'I love you Radha, I have always loved you.'

'Don't be crazy, Vijay. And never ever say that thing again to me.'

'Tell me, Radha, do you love me, or not?'

'What's wrong with you, Vijay?'

'If you will tell me to go away I will never come back again and I will break all contact with you but at least say once that you love me.'

'Come to your senses!' Radha shouted.

'I know Shyam is a rotten man you are not happy with him. Philip died in the police firing. I never killed him so why this hatred towards me? Only because I love you?'

'If you want to listen, then listen. Whatever Shyam is, he is my husband and you will never be like him because your soul is rotten. I know how Philip died but ask yourself what you did the day you were leaving for Dehradun. You think I don't know what happened that day at all. I trusted you, Vijay, and I am sure you know every little detail or would you prefer hearing it from me?'

It was too much for me to bear any further. I could feel a contraction of shame in my muscles, in my heart and something ugly was moving down my spine. It was like having the clothes torn off my body for the world to see my naked truth, and the shame was not that my body was exposed but it was because it was exposed in Radha's eyes. I was unable to withstand it; I ran away slamming the door. I quickly checked out from the hotel and reached the airport.

Sixteen

I checked in at the airport and luckily got a window seat. Soon the mighty aircraft took off, San Francisco city under my eyes, the glass of the aircraft window cold against my skin. Twenty-four hours in the flight were enough for me to go back in time and remember what Radha had meant. Her words were still echoing in my ears: *'you know the truth Vijay!'*

'Truth' – what exactly is it? What has been written in books, is that the truth? What we hear and what we see, is that the truth? It may be, it may not be. Even a correct statement may not be true unless it is complete; a partial truth is also a lie. Truth is truth what is right, what is complete and what I know. I love Radha, it is true; Philip was my friend and even that is true but only if I could have understood the difference between trust and treachery. If only I could have understood the difference between love and lust. Truth is what I know.

I now come to the most evasive and difficult part of the story, the part where I have to say how weak I am; maybe we all are that weak, who knows? It is not one incident but all the darker shades in me that gradually crept up. Now that I have lost Radha and feel unquenchable regret, if I put myself back now in the same circumstances with my conscience fully open, I am not sure whether I would do it all again or would I have the strength to refrain myself. I have been hiding the truth not from the world, not from

Radha but from myself. Today, the theory of Karma is more predominant and visible to me. Your sins come in front of you no matter what you do, what you say and however hard you try to conceal them, and today I was facing the result of my own karma. We are all humans, we all make mistakes, and we all have darker shades. A few shades come to light while others don't. I cannot blame anyone for my miseries and sufferings but myself. When I was injured, no one expected that I would survive and if God would have been kind enough, I would have died that day and my name would have been written alongside martyrs who laid down their lives for our motherland. But God had to bring me to justice and so I survived and here I am, all alone, paying for my sins.

I know I don't have a clear heart or conscience. I am a disgrace to all those who know me and I am the biggest reason why I never made any friends. I betrayed my friend the day I made a wish for his death. I betrayed the meaning of love the day lust overpowered me. I still remember my conscience screaming at me, telling me to stop, weeping out loud. But I was overpowered by my desires and I tied my conscience in chains. That day, I killed my conscience, and from that day onwards, my conscience has been killing me bit by bit.

It is only now, almost after ten years, that I can see what happened. Until now, I believed I was rational, responsible but the truth was that I had a demon inside of me, and my weakness betrayed me. The day I saw Radha, I drowned deep in her mesmerising eyes. That was the day I decided to make her mine no matter what; even Philip's friendship was not enough for me to change my mind.

Philip was my friend, a man of immense character - his identity was his purity of heart, his greatness was his concern for everyone. He was a better person than me in many ways and as I have always believed, courage was just one of them. Like physical beauty, the inner beauty of soul also attracts people towards each other, and it was evident that Radha was in love with Philip. I was unable to accept the fact; I was unable to bear the pain of losing Radha. I was a weak person, not good enough to win my love, but inside me something was burning. Every time Philip touched Radha, something simmered inside me, every time I looked into Radha's eyes I could see her eyes shining for Philip.

Finally, I had to decide: Radha or Philip? A conflict was on and I always knew the right course, but it meant a sure defeat; if not mine then definitely the defeat of my ego and a defeat of the devil in me. I had to decide and I decided that it was my life and I had to fight for it. Fight for what I believed in and I only believed in one thing – I loved Radha and I could not lose her at any cost. Grandpa had always told me that whenever one wishes for something, one must be careful because one can never know what God might grant. I wanted God to grant me my love, but till such a time that Philip was there I knew this might never happen, Radha would never be mine. I pleaded to God; I knew this would be the first and the last thing I was asking from God, and if not for all the good deeds I had done so far or will be doing in future, then he could grant me this as a reward for all the services rendered by Grandpa. I am sure Grandpa would have wept that day from the heavens above. He had always been proud of me, but that day he would have been ashamed of me. I had asked God for Philip's death. No one can believe it but my wish came true; God granted me my wish and Philip died that day in police firing. I was amazed at how soon God had heard my plea. I know all evil is born in the shadows of an evil mind and my mind was controlled by the devil in me. At the same time, I thought I was innocent, I was happy because now no one could come between Radha and me.

Love is something that cannot be acquired. Radha's love was meant for Philip and I understood now that she would love only the one whom she wants to love and she knew I was a weak person. She may have had sympathy for me but she would have never loved me. Yes, with this entire gambit there was one thing between us and that was trust. I should have understood the essence of trust; I should have understood the meaning of belief and the purity of faith. I never understood any of these things and instead, I decided to disregard all these things. More than Philip's death, what must have destroyed Radha was my breach of trust. I was selfish, entrapped in my own cocoon, and the only thing important for me was to posses Radha, I wanted her deeply, madly and obsessively. When I received my joining instructions, I knew that I would be leaving soon. I asked Radha once, twice, many times to marry me – at least an assurance that would give me the hope to live, to wait, to fight with my destiny. Radha was silent every time, she never spoke a word. I was frustrated and then the devil in me was overpowering me. Now the devil in me was working and I planned everything.

I had my depression medicines with me and I knew the effect it had. They used to render me unconscious for a good six hours. I planned to drug Radha. My conscience screamed – how could I even think about such a shameful thing and that too for Radha whom I loved? But the devil inside me had already convinced me:

You may never get the chance, and we are not attempting anything that is wrong. I just wanted to see her sleeping in front of my eyes. I just wanted to watch her for hours; I knew that after this moment I might never see her again. Radha came that night; she obviously had faith in me. I knew she would do anything to see me happy. However, my mind was somewhere else, planning on the sin I was about to commit. I dissolved the pills in her drink and waited for her to fall asleep. As soon as the pills started working, within half an hour she was in a semi-unconscious state.

I carried her to the bed and saw her sleeping; like a child, she was lying still, her head thrown back. I looked at her carefully – soft, innocent, and beautiful. I knew I could do anything at that moment. Although I just wanted to sit beside her and watch her sleep the whole night, the same devil inside me provoked me, telling me that this moment would never return and I should explore it, live it, love it and fulfill my desires. I had always been afraid of sex since there had been no one to talk about it, explain it or help me discover this mysterious world. That day, Radha's presence overpowered me, silencing my noble upbringing. My conscience disapproved, he was spitting at me, screaming at me, pleading me to stop. But the devil, the desire and the lust overpowered me.

I didn't even want the shadows to see what I was about to do. Slowly, I went towards the wall, found the switch and turned the lights off. I knew no one was watching me, not even my shadow.

Seventeen

I was back in the same city, in the same haunted three-bedroom flat, with the same distorted life. I knew nothing but one thing: there was no going back for me. I knew that this life that I had lived for so many years was now over and it has destroyed every bit of me. Vijay Amrit Raj Sharma was dead, the Radha I knew was dead and every aspect of life that I ever cherished was dead. I had absorbed disgust and pain from all sides of my existence and I was now sick of it. There was nothing left in this world that could attract me, which could give me joy, which could bring a smile on my face or tears in my eyes. I had no more wishes left; I just wanted to rest, to be dead.

I gave up my job, drank as much as I could until I was senseless. Alcohol enabled me to constantly be in an unconscious state; it did not change the truth but it kept me away from it. I achieved the new identity of an alcoholic. I could gulp down anything and everything that was laid in front of me. It was enough to drive a man out of his wits but I was unable to escape from myself. People asked me as if they were really concerned for me, but I knew their words were mocking me.

'Why do you drink so much? Is it because you are trying to forget something or are you ashamed to look people in the face?' I had no answer, I knew they were aware of the truth, my naked truth and the world was mocking me.

Often I looked at the mirror and laughed at my ugly face,

'Aye! You are a dog, and yours is a dog's life', I mocked myself. My conscience was enjoying its victory, I laughed at myself once again, spitting at my image. I was suffering and there was no cure except death. For only death could close all the chapters of my sins, leaving behind the refuge of oblivion. I wish I had enough courage to drink poison or slash my wrist. At times I would pick up the knife but on seeing my trembling hands I would throw it aside in disgust.

Therefore, I had killed my senses with alcohol. But I had plenty of wealth accumulated over the years. I knew all this money, the luxury and comforts were useless to me because they could not buy me peace of mind and a contented heart. Then I discovered something amazing – I found a new kind of thrill in gambling. This became a passion, a rage in my heart and many great gamblers feared me. I could see the fear and tremor in them whenever they saw me at the club. I gambled and put at stake huge amounts without even looking at my cards. I lost millions through gambling, all the while hating myself, mocking myself. Occasionally, when I won, I increased the stakes mercilessly. Gambling was intoxicating, more intoxicating than any brand of liquor. I'd almost lost everything but my soul was not content. I realised even if I gave away all the wealth in the world, it would not be enough penance for me to wash away my sins. Whenever I saw my face in the mirror, I hated myself and with age showing on my face and silver hair, I hated that face even more. I was now tired of gambling, ill with drinking and I was sick of myself. This way I would reach nowhere, and I decided once again to look for a different path to find a way out.

I decided to get rid of all worldly things, which had eventually become meaningless to me. I gave away my clothes and accessories to the poor, donated the left over money to orphanage homes. The only thing I was unable to part with was the watch Philip had gifted me on my twenty-first birthday. I gave away my flat to a Non Government Organization (NGO) that was giving shelter to rape victims because I was a culprit behind the same atrocities.

I decided to live like a sage, a vagabond, a nomad. I wandered from one temple to another, from one place to the other. Some gave me alms, some abused me in disgust, the street dogs barked at me, and my conscience mocked my sins and me. I fasted for many days; sometimes I ate only once a day. The flesh waned from my body, my hair and beard looking wild by now. I exposed myself to the scorching heat of the sun; I drenched myself in the cold rain until my senses grew numb. I walked barefoot on thorny bushes so that they tore my skin and blood dripped from my wounds. I tried to kill my senses, kill my memories but the pain in my heart would not subside. I tried everything – meditation, self-denial, pain, suffering, but my soul, my conscience was not at peace. My travels took me to Benaras, near the Ganges. I was told that the holy Ganges would dissolve all my sins. I sat there for days on end watching the river flow. I watched people perform all kinds of rituals from the sacred ablutions of birth, a new promise of marriage and to the last rites after death.

Benaras is like an old sage living on the banks of Holy Ganges since time immemorial. This city is older than traditions. Right from ancient times, Benaras has stood as one of the most important symbols of Hinduism, preserving the rituals and traditions of Hindu philosophy. Down the ages, pilgrims from distant lands have come to Benaras in search of divine blessings. Just like that, I was standing besides the holy Ganges in the hopes of finding a way out to wash away my sins too.

I tried to console myself that one sin, one foolish act committed could not be enough reason for all this suffering. Was it still possible to live, to breathe again in free air, to love again, to sleep again and find Grandpa's Vijay again? I closed my eyes and thought about my greatest strength. I thought about Philip, then about Radha and finally asked Grandpa to show me the way. Someone unknown, something invisible manifested itself and told me the same thing – *"the Path is the way, my son"*. I looked towards the holy waters carefully moving on, never halting and yet there, for everyone to wash their sins. It seemed like the river was telling me that everything was continuously changing – life itself was the river, flowing on and on. Sometimes it flows fast and sometimes slow. It is gentle at some places and furious at times. It can give life and at times takes away life. I realised that our mind too is like this flowing river – constantly moving on, never at rest. It has many other things dissolved in it, good and poisonous, yet it is only water, yet it is sacred, a life giver.

The flowing water had a murmuring sound and I was sure it was telling me something. I tried to comprehend but was unable to understand what it was trying to say. The red glow of the sky, like an amber curtain, crawling along the horizon painting the water in shades of orange and purple. The *ghats* were filled with thousands of people asking for forgiveness for their sins. God will forgive them, the Ganges will wash off their sins but will the Ganges be able to wash my tainted soul? I was afraid because I knew it was impossible. Even if I spend my entire life inside this holy river, my soul will never be free of the poison in me.

I ran; I wanted to escape, if not from this world then from myself. I ran towards the railway station, I changed my attire – I knew I was not a saint but an impostor. I shaved my beard, got a haircut and boarded the next train. I knew the Ganges was telling me something, and I knew it was time to wash off my sins. Where it would happen and when it would happen I had no idea, but I knew I will be free from my sins soon.

Eighteen

'Hello, brother! Hello! You! Get up! The train has reached its destination', a big, fat, Marwari *seth* was pressing on me while I was lying down on the dirty floor among the filth and muck. I was still half asleep, I raised my head a little to find out what was going on.

'*Arre bhaiya*, the train has reached its destination. Please get up! I have to pull out my luggage lying under the seat.' Passengers were hurrying, pushing on their way out. I got up with a crackling noise of groundnut shells beneath me. I dusted a handful of shells from my body. The culprits must have been passengers on the upper birth. After many days I had slept in a carefree way. Those velvet cushions and air conditioned rooms had never given me such a sound sleep as this dirty floor of the unreserved railway compartment. I didn't have any luggage with me, just a few hundred rupees in my pocket, my long unused credit card and my ex-service Identity card. I looked around and tried to make my way towards the carriage door.

I got down on an empty platform. The electronic clock over my head displayed in bright red color: 05:05. I had no idea where I was; I didn't want to know where I was heading to either. I just wanted to escape from my present life. I had boarded the first train that had caught my sight at the Benaras railway station.

I splashed my eyes with cold water; I was still drowsy. The railway station seemed deserted; people were hurrying towards their homes in auto rickshaws, cabs and their private vehicles. I moved towards the bus stand at a distance. A few buses were parked but no one was visible – no passengers, drivers or the ticket window man. From the parapet of the bus stop, the railway station was clearly visible; for a moment the place seemed familiar to me, but then I thought that all bus stops in India are almost the same. I boarded one of the buses parked in a haphazard manner and took the window seat. Still sleepy, I rested my head against the window and closed my eyes.

'Ticket… ticket, ticket please. Hello! Ticket please?' The ticket collector woke me up. I looked up, a little dazed.

'Ticket please.'

'One ticket for me', I handed a hundred-rupee note; the bus was moving.

'Where would you like to go?' the ticket collector asked.

'Wherever the bus goes.' The ticket collector gave me a baffled look.

'Here, one ticket to Mussoorie and balance, fifty rupees.'

The ticket collector moved to the Tibetan lama sitting next to me. Something struck my mind – Mussoorie. Did I hear him wrong? My sleepy eyes opened and brightened a bit. I reconfirmed with the ticket collector once again.

'This bus goes where?'

'Mussoorie', said the ticket collector, tearing another ticket from his booklet and handing it to the lama sitting next to me.

I looked outside the window; something had woken me from my sleep. My past was once again lingering on my mind.

Last night the Ganges was telling me something that I was unable to comprehend. I ran away, but the hushing sound of the river was still in my ears. I knew it was time to find the peace and solace that I was searching for all these years. I was still thinking whether I was here to pay for my sins or God was giving me another chance of penance. I looked towards the sun, peeping between the hills. I watched the snow capped mountains in the north staring at me from a distance, its allure pulling me towards itself. My grandpa's words echoing in my ears: *The path is the way...*

The bus was moving slowly uphill on the meandering roads. The cool breeze made me shiver. I glanced up and saw an eagle soaring high in the sky. It danced above the valley. It had the whole world in its arm; the sky was the limit for that eagle. I too was like him, my wings extended to the fullest in the sky. I soared higher and higher to conquer the world until my wings were broken.

I thought about the life I had lived until I had moved out of this place. I remembered everything – the *Gayatri Mantra* melting in my ears on cold winter mornings while I lay veiled inside the quilt. These were the first words I heard every morning. Ram Kumar, the millionaire *seth* from Bombay, his Kumar Villa and our small outhouse, my friend Philip and Radha.

The bus slowly came to a halt on the curling bend. The ticket collector was out of the bus, blowing his whistle, indicating the bus to move behind in the parking lot left vacant for the bus. Coolies were chasing the bus to get hold of a suitable tourist. Tourist guides displayed their hotel cards. I had a careful look at the bus stand, it was a familiar place for me; I had voyaged on Philip's motorbike everyday on this route.

Nothing had changed; everything was the same as I had left it. I climbed down and was immediately hounded by tourist guides.

'Sir! Hotel! Sir... we have off season discount and free breakfast!' the tall, lanky man gave me his hotel card.

'Sir, check out our scheme: 20 percent discount and free sightseeing', said the other one.

'Sorry brother, you've caught hold of the wrong man, I belong to this place', I handed back his card. This was amazing, I was welcomed to my place like a tourist even though looking at my attire, I neither looked like a tourist nor did my clothes indicate that I was there for holidays. Today, I was a stranger in my own land, but I did feel like I was coming home.

I walked, my footsteps taking me towards my home. It seemed like a complete age had passed by but nothing had changed over the years – the same old bus stand, the same crowd of coolies and tourists guides chasing the bus, the same old hill station where life moved at a slow pace unlike the metros where you could see everyone running. As I was walking towards home, I was thinking about whether it was possible to move back in time and change everything. I wanted to be the same old Vijay – Grandpa's angel, Philip's friend and Radha's faith.

As I approached the lane, I could see from a distance the huge iron gates and the red colored roof, the white letters outside proclaiming the bungalow: 'Kumar Villa'. On the left was the small outhouse, hidden behind the garden. My heart was pounding with an unknown fear. I wanted to bury myself in my grandpa's lap and weep, maybe Grandpa might forgive me for my sins. I wanted to cry until Philip forgave me and hugged me. I wanted Radha back in my life, not the one I desired for, but the one who was Philip's Radha.

I entered the villa from the backyard; it had the same small entrance as before. The door was closed but not locked. With shivering hands and wet eyes, I opened the door. The door opened with a rattling sound. The kitchen was empty. All I could see was dust all over and a few photographs of Lord Shiva and Lord Rama with his wife Sita, brother Lakshman and his faithful friend, Hanuman. I remembered the story my grandpa used to tell me when I was a kid. The story of Lord Rama and how he defeated the demon king Ravana. Grandpa always told me that Ravana was a great ruler, he had tremendous power but his ego became the cause of his death. He said that if God has given you power, it is to be used for universal good and not selfish deeds.

I entered the main room; it was empty but the bed and table were in its place; naked, but covered with dust. Memories echoed in my mind, especially Grandpa's hymns. I went towards the veranda and looked at Kumar Villa. The apple tree in the orchard was extending its arms, inviting the birds to come and sing a melody; flowers were blooming in the vicinity. The perimeter fence stood as if soldiers were guarding the Kumars' property. I could see a man on his haunches, plucking weeds from the flowerbeds.

'Santu *kaka*', I uttered to myself, the gardener of Kumar Villa. I moved down towards him and kept my hand on his shoulder.

'Who is it?' He looked at me, focusing his thick spectacles.

'This is a private property and trespassers will be prosecuted. Didn't you read the board outside?'

'I was looking for someone, can you please guide me?' I said, still confused. I wasn't sure if Santu *kaka* had recognised me or not.

'*Beta*, my eyes have gone weak over the years and I cannot see clearly but tell me, what are you looking for?' Santu *kaka* got up and adjusted his thick-framed spectacles again, looking at me closely.

'An old friend, Vijay used to stay in that outhouse. Do you know about his whereabouts?' I asked.

Santu touched my hand moving me closer towards him. 'I remember Pandit Bhuvnesh, but I don't recollect anything about Vijay. Was he related to him?' I was shocked and my conscience again mocked me: *See! No one knows about Vijay; they have forgotten. Your own people fail to recognise you. You don't exist anywhere – not even in your own home, your own city.*

I left from there with my head hung low, grief and shame reflecting on my face. I knew the worst that could happen was losing my identity. I went to a barber shop nearby.

'Would you help me sacrifice my hair? It's a ritual performed when a child is a year old as a mark of new life. I want to start a new life', I told the barber.

'Yes, my brother. For that we will have to go near the river. This is the first time I would be performing this ritual for an old man like you.' Both of us went to a small *ghat* near the river.

I closed my eyes and thought about my mother and then about my father. I uttered a silent prayer for them, may the Almighty God grant peace for the departed souls. I murmured the *Gayatri Mantra* to myself while the barber moved the blade on my head. After taking a dip in the cold water, I changed my attire. I wore robes of ochre like my grandpa.

'How much should I pay you?'

'I don't ask for money for this kind of job. Please pay me whatever you feel like.'

I opened my wallet and gave him everything that was in there; I didn't even count how much.

'This is all I have at the moment.'

'Thank you, sir. May God grant you peace.'

I went to the temple where my grandpa was a priest once. People were coming and going, but one thing was missing: the priest. After Grandpa's death, no priest was dedicated to take care of the temple. The Panchayat committee had appointed another priest from a local Shiva Temple, but he only came in the morning for half an hour to offer morning prayers. The manager opened the temple door at six in the morning and closed it at ten in the night. I covered my naked head with the ochre cloth covering my body. It had started to grow cold after the sunset. I pulled my knees to my chest as I sat there, shivering.

'Have some *prasad*.' I looked up; he was the same barber who had shaved my head.

'You are still here?' the barber asked me, looking a bit confused.

'I don't have a place to go to', I said, and again buried my face between my knees.

'You look like a man with lots of pain and suffering in his heart. Be my guest if it suits you', the barber sat down on his haunches, adjusting his shawl over his shoulders.

'I want to spend some time over here. Thank you for showing your concern.'

'It's very cold over here, at least keep this shawl on your body.' The barber removed the shawl from his shoulder and gave it to me.

I wrapped myself in the shawl and shrunk to one corner of the temple wall, protecting myself from the cold. I closed my eyes and thought about my grandpa.

I opened my eyes: someone held my shoulder and ran his fingers on my forehead. I raised my head and looked up. It was daylight and the sun was rising in the eastern sky. I saw my grandpa standing in front of me, covering the sun, which was directly in my face.

'Don't worry, my child. Everything will be all right. The day you left this place, everything went wrong. Now you have come back; do your duty for which God has sent you.'

'Grandpa, you are still alive!' I said, raising my head to have a clear look, my eyes still half-open. I stood up; the sun was still directly in my eyes. I tried to open my eyes but the rays of the sun were too bright for me.

'Grandpa... Grandpa...Grandpa!' I shouted. This was a similar dream I had seen when Grandpa had died, I understood that once again, Grandpa was worried about me and trying to tell me something.

'Brother, what happened? Is something bothering you?' I opened my eyes. It was the same barber with a packet of sweet meat in his hand.

'How come you are here?' I asked him.

'The whole night I was restless. I was thinking about you and felt bad that I had left you in the cold. I insist you should come to my house.' I had no place to go to but had somehow found someone in a place which was so familiar yet alien. I decided to accompany him; at least I might get something to eat.

'Brother, what is your name?' I asked, sitting on the *pyol* at the barber's house.

'My name is Hari Ram. I am from Garhwal, near Uttarkashi. I came here with my uncle seven years ago, and now after his death I'm looking after his barber shop.' He handed me a steel tumbler of hot, sweet tea.

'My wife and children stay in Garhwal. Since the past one week, there is news of heavy rains and flash floods in the upper region and I am worried about them. I want to go there as soon as the roads open up', Hari Ram sat crossed legged on the straw mat on the floor next to the *pyol*.

'Brother, what is your name? Where are you from?' asked Hari Ram.

'My name is Vijay Amrit Raj Sharma; my grandfather was the priest of the same temple where I was last night.'

'But why don't you go to your home? Why are you wandering like a nomad?' Hari Ram asked, looking a bit confused.

'I have destroyed everything – my family, my friends, their love and their faith. I had left this place years ago and now God has sent me back so that I can pay them back for my sins before I die.' I sipped the hot, sweet tea from the tumbler.

'Don't worry, brother, you may stay here as long as you want.' Hari Ram stretched his body on the mat. I stepped outside and gazed at the stars above, thinking about the vast universe. I tried to figure out the path and the way.

Nineteen

I started assisting Hari Ram at the barber shop. To do a barber's job, you require special skills, especially when one is handling the sharp blade of the razor. I was an amateur in this field so I did the job of cleaning the floor, disposing of the waste and preparing tea and food for Hari Ram. Hari Ram was a simple and honest man. He had three children: two daughters and one son. He was concerned about his family and prayed everyday for the roads to open so that he could move back to his village and assure himself that his family members were safe. When Hari Ram was with his customers, he was a thorough professional. He could talk about any subject – Bollywood movies, politics, business or cricket. Whenever some news about flash floods in the Garhwal region cropped up, he would get sad.

Then one morning, when I got up, I saw a shine in Hari Ram's eyes. He had a small bag ready for himself. He was hurrying with his morning rituals and was ready to leave.

'The roads have cleared and the first bus to Uttarkashi leaves at seven and I cannot afford to miss it. I know many like me would be waiting to go home and see their families.' Hari Ram pulled a few hundred rupees from his pocket and handed them to me.

'Keep this money until I return. In case someone inquires about me, tell them I will be back in a week or two.'

'But what will I do here all alone? I don't even know how to shave or cut hair.'

'You want to come with me to my village?' asked Hari Ram.

'Yes.'

'Then hurry up. We need to catch the first bus at any cost.'

The bus was already jam-packed and there was no space left for us. All the seats were occupied. In fact, there was no space to stand either and the driver refused to take in more people due to safety concerns. The next bus was at two o' clock in the afternoon and we were sure there would be no space on that bus either. Hari Ram was obviously sad. I felt sorry for him, feeling helpless.

Then, something struck my mind – I could see a convoy of Army trucks lined up. I figured they would be going to the same location to provide relief to the affected areas. I inquired with a few drivers and they confirmed that the convoy was moving to Uttarkashi. I requested them for help, but they told me to take permission from the convoy commander, *Subedar* Dharampal. The name sounded familiar. I went to meet the convoy commander. Times had changed, appearances had changed but the fearless eyes of the then *Havildar* Dharampal, my sniper, were still the same. I recognised him but it took a while for him to recognise me. Life is like a river, which goes by comes back to you.

I greeted Dharampal but his weird look towards me confirmed that he needed an introduction.

'Many years ago, you were with me in Surankote, Jammu and Kashmir. You were the best shooter we had and it was your bullet that knocked down Abu Ali. Do you recognise your injured company commander?'

Astonished, Dharampal looked into my eyes. 'Are you Vijay *Saab*?' He asked in a surprised tone. I smiled back acknowledging.

'It would have been hard to recognise you if you wouldn't have taken me down memory lane.' He hugged me. 'I salute you, sir, from my heart. I know, once upon a time you were a valiant soldier.' I laughed at the mention of the word 'valiant' and thought at least someone is there to identify me and still have a good opinion about me. 'You've changed a lot, sir.'

'Many things have changed, Dharampal. Many people have changed. Look at you now – a *Subedar*.'

'Yet, memories are still the same', added Dharampal.

Dharampal was more than happy to help us. He gave Hari Ram and me a special place in his vehicle. We talked about our amazing days in the counter insurgency operations. I asked about my unit and what had been happening over the years. The convoy moved along the winding curves of the narrow road by the river, swirling like a serpent, until we reached Uttarkashi. By the time we reached Uttarkashi, it was already dark. We stayed at the makeshift transit camp for Army convoys. When the day began, we bid farewell to Dharampal and moved towards Hari Ram's village. The solitary bridge connecting the main road and the mule track to the village was washed away in the flash flood. The river flowing beneath us was beautiful as well as furious. A Bailey bridge constructed by the Army and the locals helped us to cross the river.

'I thank you, Vijay', spoke Hari Ram. 'It is because of you that I was able to reach home. I never knew you were an ex-army man.'

'In fact, I should thank you. I was homeless and without a friend. I have found a friend in you, Hari Ram.' He was like Philip, I thought. Even Dharampal was like Philip; all are like Philip – good at heart, pure from within.

At about noon, we reached Hari Ram's village. The mud cottages had been reduced to earth, the streets were deserted, even the dogs weren't barking. The entire village had been washed away in the flash floods. At the end of the village, on the path that led through to a stream, a young girl's body lay there, smeared in mud. When we moved closer, there were two more bodies. I realised the entire village had been washed away. Hari Ram looked at me with gloomy eyes; he also realised the same thing. He went down on his knees and started weeping like a child.

I consoled him, 'Hari Ram, till the time you see it with your own eyes, don't believe anything.' I knew only God could help us at that juncture.

'We will request the Army officials to search for your family; we must check the nearest relief camp', I said, while Hari Ram sobbed.

The valley by the river seemed like a haunted island. There was an eerie silence and the stink of rotting bodies filled the area, which once would have been lively and bustling with devotees of *Devbhoomi*. Nature's fury had left behind a trail of devastation in this temple valley. Thousands of people and many structures had vanished without a trace. The silence was occasionally broken by the sound of army choppers scouting for survivors, and journalists taking stock of the situation. The survivors recounted how they saw people, their belongings, cattle and even vehicles being swept away by the ravaging water. The story of devastation was repeated everywhere. With entire road networks washed away at many places, the Army had set up rescue camps wherever possible. One such camp was the GR military base on the banks of the river near Hari Ram's village, Bhatwada. Around one thousand people descending from nearby villages and other areas had camped here. The Garhwal Rifles battalion of the Army had turned their barracks into a temporary camp for stranded tourists. From the GR military base, some pilgrims were sent on choppers to safer areas while others were encouraged to trek down a 30-km temporary road built by the Border Roads Organization.

That same evening, we reached the GR military base camp across the river. Hari Ram kept the photograph of his wife and three children in his hand and pleaded everyone that came his way to have a look at the photograph, and whether they had seen them anywhere. We requested the Army officials numerous times and gave them complete details but Hari Ram's family could not be traced. There were many who were still missing; in fact, finding dead bodies was a challenging task as well.

The next day, the Army ordered a rescue team to evacuate those who were alive, but I knew it was probably too late to find anyone alive over there. They recovered the three bodies that we had seen. After searching the area further, twenty more bodies, buried under the debris were recovered. Hari Ram's family was still missing.

After five days, the hope to find Hari Ram's family was diminished. I knew we would never find them. Hari Ram knew he would never see them, not even one last time. He was unable to perform the last rites, a burning pyre for their souls to rest in peace. Hari Ram had started behaving like a lunatic, he would hold his hands, wipe his tears and run to scan the newly recovered dead bodies.

'What was my crime? What sins had my children committed that I had to face this? I don't know why God has punished me', Hari Ram complained. The situation was helpless, so weak that even I lacked words to encourage him or console him.

We decided to move back to Mussoorie, at least there was some hope of life there. Then, for the last time we entered Hari Ram's village. We looked at each other; I knew Hari Ram wanted to stay there, he could feel his memories, the touch of his family in his heart and his hope buried in the soil beneath his feet. I could feel his sorrow. This was the first time I could feel for someone, indeed anyone. Ego is the synonym of evil and selflessness meant virtue; similarly, repentance is the way to redemption. I have nothing in me but pain and here I decided to bear the pain of others so that I could free myself of my own inflicted pain. All these years I knew only my sorrow, only my pain, but today my heart was in agony – as much as Hari Ram's heart. That day, I knew I had a goal. I knew I had to stay here and I knew I had to rebuild this village for a friend, for Hari Ram. In Hari Ram I could see Philip. Yes, he was like Philip.

Twenty

I understood the basic essence of life: life should be simple, with small goals. 'Build' was an important word with an intense meaning. When I was a child, my grandpa was building me into a good human being; Radha and Philip helped me build a loving relationship of trust and friendship. When I was in the Army, it was important to build hope and morale during times of difficulty. I realised it was time to build everything in me: my character, my faith, my morale and my hope. I knew it would start by building this village once again. I had promised myself that this village would live again. The biggest question though, was where to begin? Rebuilding an entire village was not an easy task.

It was time to move back in time and revise what I had learnt over the years, especially what the Army had taught me: teamwork. I needed two basic things to start with – first was money and the second were volunteers to help me. I had millions of rupees in my bank account when I had come back from San Francisco but I had lost everything in clubs, alcohol, gambling and whatever that was left I had given away to charities. Now, at this juncture, when I desperately needed the money I was realising my foolishness and wished I had saved something for the future. The only money I had was my Army pension that was regularly deposited in my bank account every month. Of course that was not enough, but one must begin with or without financial backup, with people joining hands or not.

I had a purpose in my mind and I knew I was doing it not for myself but for Hari Ram.

We decided to look for volunteers to join us. We checked the relief camps, Hari Ram found fifteen people from his village. I had fifteen people to start my rebuilding mission, and after including Hari Ram and myself, the number increased to seventeen.

We worked the way I was taught in the Army: food and accommodation were immediate requirements. We managed to get some food packets from the relief camp, which would last for two days so the priority was to establish our own cook-house. We also procured five tents from the rehabilitation camp. With the supplies on our backs, we marched towards the village.

After we established a cook-house, we pitched the tents – a makeshift arrangement until we were able to rebuild basic amenities in the village. Women and children were assigned to manage the cook-house while the others were assigned to clear the debris. Hari Ram was given the responsibility to cater for basic things like rations, utensils, and kerosene oil and to also convince more people to join us. The progress was obviously very slow – it would take us months to clear off the entire area. Most families that joined us, continued to struggle with their daily needs, clean water, basic health care and food. The sense of loss and despair prevailed for a long time. At times, I did feel the hope dying but I admonished the thought every time. I was determined and I would not give up until I win or I'd die trying.

We requested the Army to help us to clear the debris and within a week, most of the debris were cleared. I was happy that at least we had something to start off with. The news of our rebuilding mission had traveled far after the Army helped us clear the area. Now more and more people were willing to join us. A majority of them were people who had some association with the village. Within two months, changes were visible in the form of a few huts and a well-established cook-house. Even more people joined in and the strength increased to eighty. I remember I had the same strength under me when I was a company commander. I divided them into sections, each section consisting of ten people, working towards various aspects of the rebuilding project.

The new developments had given us new hope and now we could plan, we could think. I evaluated that there would be four aspects on which our mission would get going: first was the infrastructure, second livelihood, third consolidation and the fourth was the most important, especially for the future generations – education.

Money had never had any importance in my life, but today I realised that money was a necessary evil. The next thing on the agenda was to do something so that the village people could get some employment and they could become self-sufficient. I also wanted to open a school for children; there was no future without education. I wrote to the chief minister requesting him for two favors: first to link the village with the main highway, and second, to set up the infrastructure for a high school that could later be upgraded to intermediate. I also made detailed plans: a short term plan for five years and a long term plan for ten years and forwarded my proposal to the chief minister's office. I explained what I had planned to do and how I was visualizing things to move.

We had thought of a four-point project released in phases for Bhatwada village. First was to develop the infrastructure, including road networks, dwelling units, schools, health care facilities, banking and other essential services. They all existed previously but were scattered. The second stage would begin once the infrastructure had been created – the village would require state transport corporation connectivity, a Government health care department, Education resources for children, wireless and P&T services, electricity, clean water supply and other basic amenities.

After these two stages, we would have a platform to grow further and the third phase would begin only after five to six years though, once the base was set up. It would explore avenues for business and employment – both government based and independent. The main aim was to create livelihood in the village itself so that people didn't have to leave the place in search for a brighter future. Simultaneously, it would also aim for consolidation and improving upon the created assets with newer, advanced technologies and further exploring the avenues to make it a model village at par with American and European villages. The aim would be to attract companies to explore markets related to finance, IT, tourism, agriculture, natural resources and adventure sports. I knew that the vision will eventually be a reality because cities had limited scope of expansion and growth; future developments would definitely take place in villages.

I never expected that my projection would be viewed so seriously, but to my surprise, my requisition was looked into and within a month a project was released to connect Bhatwada village with the state highway under the scheme called *Pradhan Mantri Gram Sadak Yojna*, or the Prime

Minister's Village Road Development Scheme. This was the first time I realised that things do move at government offices, the only requirement was to approach them in the right way. The project for building the high school was also passed. The advantage was that many of the villagers were employed in the road building and school infrastructure project; they had employment of their own. Subsequently, other projects for banking facilities, P & T, health care, and roadways were also sanctioned as a five year plan and other things that I had projected were mentioned in the long term perspective planning in the next ten years.

I had a vision and the vision was that the future generations should have a bright future. More importantly, they must build everything here rather than go exploring opportunities in Europe, America or other metropolitan cities.

Within a span of five years, the village had managed to change completely. From a village where everyone lived in poverty, Bhatwada was emerging as a model village in remote locations of hills. This was achieved through sustainability and people's participation. It was the result of how the right kind of efforts could bring about miracles and also attract people back into its fold who had preciously left for lack of opportunities. One such name was Professor Amit Uniyal, the Vice Chancellor at Doon University. I knew professor Uniyal would be the key to my vision of education. I was planning for three major developments to take place: setting up a digital infrastructure to provide e-awareness and literacy to the community, developing an integrated sustainable model for education and lastly, giving the future generation a platform to compete with the rest of the world.

Twenty One

Education was still my prime concern and Professor Uniyal was the man who would definitely have an answer to all my queries. Professor Uniyal was an icon in the Garhwal region; he had a life long interest in education and its significance in life. Professor Uniyal was the Vice Chancellor of the esteemed Doon University that had provided career-based courses for future employment to students of the Garhwal region. Before this University was established, students were forced to explore avenues outside this region for professional employment opportunities. Professor Uniyal had also authored half a dozen books regarding his dream vision about education and its impact and real meaning of right education.

Professor Uniyal's views about education were that it should provide holistic and integral touching upon physical, emotional and aesthetic developments in addition to academics. For him education was not learning, but it was individual freedom. The aim was to free every individual from the greed of reward and it was proposed that no ranking system would prevail in our system; the aim was not to establish a large school but we wanted a limited number of students in every class with right kind of teachers. In case a student was excelling in sports then we would like to concentrate on his sporting ability rather than encouraging him to solve numeric problems.

Professor Uniyal agreed to visit our village; it was time now to turn his vision into reality. After making his assessment, he agreed to pool in his resources to create a model education system at Bhatwada. He requested a fair amount of budget to be released for making state of the art infrastructure, model rooms and e-learning provisions for the village. He also assured the government that it would be on trial basis and in case the project is successful, the same model would be implemented in other schools. His project was named Gurukul, which will offer a revolutionary concept in early childhood education that develops multiple intelligences of a child and promotes all development. It also included interactive curriculum in scientifically designed classrooms to suit the different learning, giving flexibility to the adapt child's developmental needs. The facilities that Gurukul provides are ample, like digital classrooms, inventive learning laboratories, career guidance and counseling centers, audio-visual rooms and field trip excursions. Fee was minimal and opportunities ample which flooded the school with children in no time. The only problem we were facing was eligible teachers, especially for classes post high schools.

Professor Uniyal had a solution up his sleeves: he made it mandatory for new recruitment of professors to do a six months probation in remote areas. Their performance was based on results of students and if they were not up to the required level, the probation was increased to another six months. No two individuals are same, they think differently and they act differently. Similarly the teachers were of different kinds. Some took it as a punishment and counted their probation days while some were willing to see the problem, understand it and displayed enthusiasm. They never created hindrances and attempted to solve many problems of existence at their respective levels, a few also volunteered to serve there for longer duration.

Education or the right kind of education brought everyone to identify the difference in personal gains and collective success. The personal success was accidental, momentary while every success was counted as a collective effort. Soon the vision was visible, we were creating doctors, engineers, sports person, IT experts, but none projected his or her achievement as his personal gain, the word Gurukul was before them and a vision to see beyond self was in their acts. We avoided the concept of competition and mutual destruction but encouraged to learn meaning of life and the art of collective survival. We never created machines but developed human beings who were integrated and therefore intelligent, it helped us discover lasting values. We never blamed the child for his failure but it was counted as the failure of teachers and parents.

Soon Gurukul became a symbolic mark of inspirational education, our students excelled in every field not just across the state but also nationwide. We gave them an international platform to learn, but only to develop their skills and not to become a slave and dedicate their efforts to earn in dollars or pounds. Professor Uniyal's retirement soon after meant that he came back to his village and became the chief controller of the Gurukul Education system. He was a visionary and was glad to see his efforts giving added dividends. He always used to tell me,

'Vijay, I always wanted to see my village the way I see it today, but I never had the courage to work for it. I fled my village when I was young in the hope to find a new life somewhere else and now when I am about to die, I have come full circle.'

Professor Uniyal's son was working in London and he refused to come to his native village, but I was sure that soon

Bhatwada would be better than any place in the world, be it for infrastructure, quality of life, education or excellence. Two years after his retirement, Professor Uniyal passed away but he had already given us a platform to continue his efforts.

Years passed by but we were engrossed in our work. I don't know whether all my efforts were enough to wash away my sins but I knew I would serve this village until my very last breath. However, a wish, an agony, a pain remained; I wanted it to subside. Every evening, I would listen to the river, it was telling me something: *"It's not enough, Vijay. Continue, move on like me every moment, every day."*

In the darkness I would gaze at the stars trying to find my universe, looking up for help, for support from Grandpa and Philip. I know they are watching over me from the heavens above. At lonely nights I would dream about Radha and ask her to forgive me for my sins. I don't know if it was ever enough.

Twenty Two

I continued my research work on the future avenues that could be explored in this particular area. I took the help of research institutes and other NGOs to find out the kind of avenues that could be explored in this area. Two things were predominant that can bring change: first was tourism and the second was to figure out a way to use the enormous energy that was prevalent in the river. The hydel power project was the answer. After the calamity, tourism had suffered a major bolt, This was a religious region and had tourists visiting every year but now we could hardly see them; they were scared. We tried to revive tourism based on religious grounds but were unsuccessful. Religious tourism had a limited scope for growth but yes, a hydel power project had plenty of scope for collective development. The proposal was sent across and soon a government based hydel power project was launched in the vicinity.

People were motivated and had seen hope and new opportunity knocking their doors. The hydel power project not only gave more employment opportunities but also resolved the electricity problem of the entire area. Now there was electricity 24 hours a day, without any power cuts. Then I had new plans. I proposed trekking and mountaineering clubbed with adventure sports like Para gliding and bungee jumping. For this, I selected teenagers who had the capability to explore adventure sports. Initially, I trained them at adventure school Kasauli and later opened a similar institute to train others in this location. I tried to get a little publicity and within a year, our adventure sports business had taken off way beyond our expectations.

I also understood that the economy would rest mostly on small scale industries and if we have bigger players or a few leading brand names backing us then things will not be difficult. I revived my contacts and needed someone to invest in my plans of small scale industries. I had planned to set up a firm manufacturing products of Ayurveda. The possibility of opening such a firm was positive due to rich flora and fauna available for production of organic food and Ayurveda. We also explored the opportunity of manufacturing local handicraft that was in high demand in many places of our country. I got a sponsor who was helping us not because he wanted to generate profit but as a welfare measure to help rural areas. In the initial years of setup we had an annual turnover of rupees four hundred thousand which was just enough to sustain our small scale industry projects for the future.

My aim was to provide the entire village community with decent housing with generous space, plenty of jobs and integral social amenities. The idea was to provide a platform that led to other developments to prosper. This idea also stimulated shared values and a pride in the local environment. This sense of common responsibility for the public realm has been the sole reason for our success. Slowly, the small-scale industries showed improved results, the key result areas were Ayurveda medicines and organic farming. We established modern sampling plants and state of the art packaging facilities. Sponsors realised the scope of gaining profit from these industries and they pumped more finances and added more infrastructure.

Time went on and my dream was turning into a reality. I was growing old with each passing day, and so was Hari Ram. Nights were generally our time for peace. We sit outside and gaze at the stars trying to discover our own world. The afternoons were busy with some or the other issue at hand, but every evening we would sit together, listen to the sound of the river, say our prayers and have dinner together. I know Hari Ram was still trying to find his wife and children in the flowing currents of the water and I was still searching for my redemption. Hari Ram now owns a hi-tech salon in Bhatwada, our trekking assignments are now booked worldwide through the Internet and our organic products are exported to twelve nations across three continents. Money flowed in and there were ample opportunities for education, employment and cohesive development.

Bhatwada was now recognised as one of the most advanced places in India. Recently, the Discovery channel team was here to find out how a village that had almost entirely washed away in the flash floods had grown into an advanced hub of small-scale industries, organic farming and adventure sports activities. They covered the entire program for over a month and understood our concept of cohesive development and our vision of education at the Gurukul.

They approached me for an interview appointment and I agreed. I explained to them how things began, but I never told them why. I told them how years ago, when I came here first, nothing was there, then there was a vision and it was only because of the blessings of the Almighty that we were able to achieve whatever was visible today.

I asked them about the telecast of their program, would it be broadcast in India only or world wide. I know it was a stupid query but I had Radha on my mind and that maybe some day she would see this program. They told me that the program initially would be broadcast only in India and later, depending on its success and viewership might be broadcast globally. I was happy that at least some hope is prevalent, that some day Radha might view this program and appreciate my efforts, and forgive me and accept me.

I am now an old man, nearly seventy-years-old. Hari Ram is also old and feeble like me but till date he can give you a perfect haircut at his salon. I realised that I have been old and decrepit for so many years and today there was nothing left in me but old age. With every passing moment, the only urge I craved was to feel better about myself, the only thing I wanted was my conscience to accept me. Today Hari Ram told me that my name had been listed for a national award. I laughed because the award was not important but the recognition was. I know I am symbolic, only a propagator, the efforts were collective one. It is true the most important thing is to feel good about yourself without the approval of someone else. You have to feel worthwhile and acceptable in your own eyes, so that you'll be able to look confidently into the eyes of people around you.

Tonight again I stared at the sky looking at the stars and the heavens above, trying to locate my universe, trying to find Philip, Grandpa and Radha, only to make a wish that they were with me at this moment. Philip and Grandpa I am sure and I know; yes, I know they would be looking from the skies above, but what about Radha? Was she alive or resting peacefully and watching from the skies above? I don't know. The day I left San Francisco I neither inquired about her nor made any contact with her. If she was a lustful desire then she had to die and because she was love I remembered her with every painful breath I have been taking all these years. But today again, I had a desire and this will be my last desire I know. I wanted Radha to know, maybe she would forgive me and love me because no matter what I was or what I did, the truth remains unmoved that I always loved her from the core of my heart, and all this heart has inside are bitter-sweet memories.

Epilogue

The National award for a new vision of hope was announced today. I was selected for my achievement for creating a new infrastructure in Bhatwada village and Professor Uniyal's concept of a Gurukul school in rural areas. The date of the investiture ceremony at the Rashtrapati Bhawan, The President's House was fixed. I requested for passes for my students and requested for two additional VIP passes. I posted these VIP passes to Radha and Shyam. It was important for me that she should know, even if she was unwilling to attend the ceremony.

I cannot say why God choose me for the work I did, or whether He wanted me to wash my sins, but today I was at peace. I had learned something, and for me the world had been transformed. Today I had been liberated and had the courage to look into the eyes of the whole world. Beautiful and delighted, it was to face the world. Different were the sun, the air and the moon. Today I heard a voice, a voice in my own heart. Today I was proud of myself, and this was good, this was necessary.

The day I was awarded the National Award, I was asked to deliver a speech about my achievement. I had no idea what to say, where to start and thought it would have been wise to come prepared with a speech. I stood by the steps of the podium, the audience looked at me. I remembered the misery of the moment when I want to choose the right words but my fear to face the audience was depriving me of the right words.

'Today it is indeed an honor to stand at this podium and accept your felicitation with pride. From my heart I thank you all, and to my students I tell them that I will be happy to see them excel and hear anything good about them. I never had a name and it took a lifetime for me to make a name. People may not remember me tomorrow, but yes, my friends and people who have loved me at any stage of life will always be proud of me. I am not the only one, the brain behind the concept was Professor Uniyal who left us but not before creating a new vision for future education. He deserved this award more than me. Alone, I am nothing and this award I accept on behalf of the entire Bhatwada village.

'Throughout the centuries, man has invented new hope and gave a new vision to mankind. I am neither a visionary nor a creator but a man searching for a way to escape from himself. I have been an ordinary man throughout my life. I have made mistakes, some which were acceptable and some, which were not. I had a deep wound in my heart and it burned inside me for many years until today when I feel my wounds are healed. I found friendship but was soon lost in the dark shadows of greed and hatred. I wanted to explore love but my overwhelming desire of lust had betrayed a loving man inside me. Then I blamed my fortune and thought why don't I? Even bad people have good fortunes, even they have friends and even they have love in their lives. My conscience had eaten my peace of mind because of one sin I committed years ago. One incident in my life changed everything. I was searching for the truth, a permanent one, which would satisfy me with absolute tranquility.

'I came across many people in life; all were ordinary with shades of black as well as white. I understood one thing: all were good at heart and all were sinners. All were ordinary like me, childlike people, businessmen, army men, traders, teachers, employees, workers they all were same; like me. They made me understand that they all love their children, all have a hidden desire of lust inside them, they all crave for money, they all admire the strong and the beautiful and they all want to be successful in life. Like I say they all want to make a name for themselves. What made me different from them was that I understood the foolishness of a mind laden with desires, and that was the turning point in life, that was the knowledge I attained which was indeed wisdom. Faith in karma. It is your karma that is in front of you today or a day will come when you will have to face your karma. You cannot hide from your karma, so might as well face them. We must trust in God and follow the path shown by him, do your duty faithfully and move on with a mantra: path is the way. This theory of Karma I had understood from the holy Gita. One book I would recommend all my students to read.

'Another basic thing The Holy Gita made me understand was the importance of action. A man cannot enjoy respite from activity by non undertaking of actions, nor can he obtain success by surrendering them. What is action? This question is still a point for contention even for the learned ones. Action must be understood and it must have a positive effect on humanity, on your character development and your confidence. Mis-action must also be understood, God may grant you fruit for your mis-actions, but be assured you may not be strong enough to face the consequences. Similarly, inaction also needs to be understood, you may think and think for an entire lifetime, keep wishing and praying God to fulfill your desires but without action nothing will move, things will remain the way they are.

'Some people need love and admiration to come to the threshold of success, some need ambition stronger and larger than life; I needed my sins. There was a constant conflict within me, and with the aim of self-forgetfulness, I turned to gambling, alcohol and other mysterious and fanciful religious doctrines. It was only later that I understood that all I need is to face my sins and more importantly accept my sins and not glorify ways to escape. I understood that the only possible way to eliminate the conflict in my mind was to accept it. There seems no difference to me in good or bad, holiness and sins are similar to me and beauty and ugliness are alike. Today, I can assure myself that the evil in life is a transitory that should be treated like an accident. We must believe that God is our father, and we must trust him. What counts is the acceptance of truth and realisation at heart, which gives you the determination to do the right what your conscience demands from you. I have come across such a stage in life where I can say that I needed sins to do something worthwhile for someone. I needed lust to understand the depth of love, I required the desire of possession and most shameful despair to understand what hope actually means. Desire; what is it? Yes, it is the root cause of evil, therefore self control is the mantra and the way out. To quote the Holy Gita:

"The self should raise the self, should not lower the self.
For the self is verily the friend of the self, and the self is verily the enemy of self.
The self is the friend of that self, by which self the self is conquered;
But to one, conquered by the non self, the self moves in enmity as a foe"

'Everything is here, the reason I do not believe in the two-world theory of heaven and hell. Good, bad, ugly everything is inside you, see it with utmost care whom you are willing to accept. Heaven and hell are right in front of you. You will feel the essence of heaven in every holy deed you perform and you will feel your conscience burn in the fire of hell in every sin you perform after killing your conscience.

'Everything in my life had taught me something or the other, but three people had taught me everything that I understand today. I had a friend Philip, who taught me the difference between hatred and friendship, Radha, the one whom I love the most, she taught me what desire is, what lust was, and more importantly, the meaning of love. She gave me the wisdom that love cannot be acquired or stolen. She will give the sweet fruit of love to the one whom she wants to give. The Army taught me the essence of karma, the path to duty, never say die attitude. Every individual I came across told me that we all are the same, a little ugly but beautiful, full of greed yet large at heart and most importantly we are full of desire of lust yet we require only love.

'Among all these my grandfather gave me the biggest lesson, he showed me the way and told me- The Path is the Way itself. He was with me like a flowing river on the move always, yet always at the same place. He told me to move on but be there, never leave your conscience behind. He taught me the essence of life and I leave all my students with something that my grandfather used to tell me when I was a school kid:

Tu to dariya hai apni manzil dhoond hi lega,
Rastae to karwan ko chaiyae
Tu behta ja ganga ki tarah.

You are like a flowing river that will make its own way. The roads are for the others. Keep moving ahead like a flowing river.

The path is the way.'

The central hall of Rashtrapati Bhawan, The President's House, echoed with sounds of applause as I finished my speech; with weak feeble legs I moved out of the limelight still thinking about my journey to this stage. Yes, it has been a long journey and a tiresome one at that. Today I really feel tired and I realise I am a weak feeble old man, almost seventy years old, and it took three decades to reach this landmark, to wash away my sins and most importantly to let my conscience accept the Vijay in me. Today I understood the meaning of Vijay and why grandpa had given me this name Vijay, which means the victorious one.

The same night after the investiture ceremony when I slept, I had a dream. Radha was standing in front of me, the same Radha whom I love, the same face that I had seen for the first time in college, dressed in a red *salwar kameez*. I looked at her and asked. Why have you forsaken me? You feel I am still a sinner, untrustworthy, sly character and full of cruel intentions? At this she embraced me, wrapped her arms around me and pulled me close to her chest and kissed me. I know she had forgiven me; her love was her faith in me. That night I slept the way I had always desired, one which finally put my soul at peace.

ACKNOWLEDGEMENTS

I thank Swati Joshi for her support, Swastika Bist for cover design and Jayant Karna for the cover image. I would also like to thank the editorial team for their assistance. I would also like to thank my wife Pragati for her detailed and honest comments on the work.

ALSO BY THE AUTHOR

Crossroads

By Mohit Badoni

Major Rajesh Singh is a decorated soldier with two gallantry awards to his name – Shaurya Chakra and Sena Medal. During his college days, he discovers friendship and is smitten by love only to lose both at the crossroads of his life. Defeated and dejected, he leaves home to begin a new life in Rajpur, a small village nestled in the foothills of Mussoorie. There, he forges a new friendship, bonds amongst the local people he encounters and most importantly, meets Diya who instils a new hope and revives the languishing flames of love. But rarely do two eyes dream about the same thing. Fate beckons him to loftier goals and he is commissioned in the Indian army where he battles against anti-national elements and exhibits prodigious courage and fortitude. After receiving his second gallantry award, however, he decides to quit the Army and move back to Mussoorie where he has lived his best and worst days. He quits not because he is a misfit in the Army, but because he wants to embark on a spiritual journey towards redemption and fulfillment.